The Face of Agamemnon

The Face of Agamemnon

JOHN GALWAY

authorHOUSE®

AuthorHouse™
1663 Liberty Drive
Bloomington, IN 47403
www.authorhouse.com
Phone: 1-800-839-8640

Published by AuthorHouse   03/25/2013

ISBN: 978-1-4817-8785-7 (sc)
ISBN: 978-1-4817-8786-4 (hc)
ISBN: 978-1-4817-8787-1 (e)

This novel is based on a story related in the course of an interview conducted for a national Irish radio (RTE) programme in1984 with the putative leader of the Estonian Resistance during World War II.

This story I subsequently began to research with a view to publication but found that I was unable to verify it conclusively.

The man interviewed died about two years later, leaving me a manuscript purporting to be the complete story.

Further research, however, opened up quite a different perspective from which a former lieutenant began to emerge as the main protagonist.

If his story could be verified, and it seems impossible now, it would connect him with one of the great thefts of ancient art perpetrated during World War II.

It would also connect him with an international incident that severely strained relations between the Russian authorities and Germany in 1993 when a number of these stolen items were displayed in Moscow's Pushkin Museum.

⊙⟩⟨⊙

Estonia, 1939-45

Tallinn, Estonia, 20 June 1940, 1.00 a.m.

Mycenae, Greece, 1876: In November of that year, retired millionaire businessman and amateur archaeologist Heinrich Schliemann—the discoverer of Troy—wrote to the king of the Hellenes. He told him that in the tombs of Mycenae he had found "immense treasures of the most ancient objects of pure gold" and that it was his intention to "give them intact to Greece."

He registered his deep satisfaction and sense of fulfillment by ending the letter with these words: "I have gazed upon the face of Agamemnon."

Chapter 1

ᕮᕮᕮᕮᕮ

THE SKY OVER Tallinn never becomes completely dark in midsummer, not even after 1.00 a.m. There was enough light for the three men to move quickly across the shunting yard of the Baltic Station, out of sight of the NKVD men waiting in the darkened main building. They climbed to the roof of the locomotive shed as the train rolled softly nearer, pulling up with a discreet squeal of brakes.

From the parapet above, they could see everything. Shale-oil smoke drifted lazily skyward from the engine. At intervals between the carriages, they could make out the open boxcars, thick with Russian soldiers, silent and still, waiting. Two or three climbed down. Their boots crunched gravel, going down the tracks. Dim lights came on in the main building. The NKVD men began to detach from the shadows. It was like a silent play, well rehearsed. That's how Aleks Kallas described it to me.

It was 20 June 1940. Three days previously, the Russians had invaded Estonia. The three men on the roof—Aleks Kallas, Johann Semmal, and Peeter Sirel, future leaders of the resistance—were about to witness the deportation of the entire legally constituted government of their country.

First, they heard shuffling feet coming down the tracks, eventually emerging into the pool of light. They saw the pathetic procession of women, led by the Prime Minister's wife, stumbling over the stones in high heels, tightly clutching the hands of children. There were at least 120 of them, devoid of luggage, flanked by armed guards. The NKVD men moved in, packing them roughly on board. There was only the whimpering of children, doors being slammed, and then silence. In the sinister hiatus, steam hissed. Down the line, echoing hollowly, hammers tapped wheels and pistons.

Forty minutes passed before the second stumbling procession—some 100 government ministers, politicians, and senior civil servants—came down the line. There was a loud groan from someone on discovering his family on board. Doors slammed shut in rapid succession, a whistle blew, and slowly, the wheels began to turn. Soon the train was a distant rumble down the tracks. None of the watchers spoke. They listened for a long time. The steam whistle called forlornly in the distance and was immediately snatched away by the wind.

Aleks Kallas was convinced it was the end of everything. It might have been but for the anger which began to consume his entire being.

In retrospect, it seemed that Johann Semmal's fate began to unravel that night in a sequence of events that culminated in his seemingly inevitable death in 1956.

Peeter Sirel had very definite ideas about fate and inevitability. He claims he cheated the fate laid out for him in 1991. I know now that he is psychic. It was his strange power and knowledge which took me again and again to see him in Finland. He was eighty-nine last time I saw him and ninety by my next visit. And to think I almost missed that story. I would have missed it if Aleks Kallas had not escaped to Sweden in 1944. I would have missed it anyway had I not been standing on the deck of a barge in Ireland in the winter of 1984, talking to an old friend. It started so casually, so slowly . . .

I was back in my home town, changing my life, or maybe putting it back together. The man on the deck of the wheelhouse was Sid Reid, doyen of river-dwellers. I'd known him all my life. It was time for me to go home after hours of talking. I didn't want to, because we were watching a sunset on the lake.

"Since you're a writer," said Sid, "why don't you go and meet this fellow Kass?"

"You mean the Estonian Resistance leader? Is that a true story, do you think?"

That's how it all started. Of course, at this stage, we didn't know him as Aleks Kallas. Because with the issue of Swedish (Aliens) Passport Reg. Numbers 5865/44/46280/38590 on 2 November 1944, he had become Arthur Kass, Displaced Person, who arrived in Ireland three years later on a temporary work permit.

"Is he still running the boat-repair yard?"

"That closed down. Now he's in antiques."

On a bleak afternoon in January 1985, I met Arthur Kass for the first time, in his workshop down by the river.

We stood in the cold, draughty shed, gazing down at the clock I had taken in to be repaired. It had been placed on a rickety table among the shavings, cannibalized clocks, and beautiful bits of antique furniture. Smells of oil, resin, and glue confounded my senses. Kass had the disconcerting habit of standing perfectly still, staring intently, and waiting for any newcomer to introduce or explain himself. I stated my business, and he let his gaze fall once more on the clock.

"Was it going when you got it?" It was the first time he'd spoken.

"Oh, yes," I said.

He was in shirtsleeves, while I huddled into a warm jacket. In a dusty corner, an ancient electric heater ate up the oxygen. A breeze from an open window stirred the shavings. Kass was of medium stature, with pale, Russian-type features. The voice was husky and resonant.

"So?" he asked. It somehow seemed like a challenge.

3

"I overwound it," I said truthfully. I then added, "That seemed to snap a wire holding the weights."

He looked at me.

"Do you know something about clocks?"

I had to keep him talking, I thought, so I rattled on a bit about the bits I'd learned, feeling my way with him. He was looking down at the clock, rubbing it gently with his hand. His eyes came up and fixed me with such a look that I trailed off. It was as if I had received a quick, stabbing pain in my solar plexus. He knew I was lying, pretending, making it up.

"Can you come back next week?" he asked quietly.

"What day?"

"Tuesday, but phone me first." He handed me a grubby card.

With that, I left. It was that look more than anything else which got me interested in Arthur Kass.

In the weeks that followed, I learned that Kass had written an account—still an unpublished manuscript—of his experiences in the resistance. He knew I was a writer, but he was reluctant at first to let me read it. A phone call I received from Finland changed all that. It was from my old friend Tapio Koskela, asking me to give an intensive or "full-immersion" English language course to a business colleague of his. I had done this abroad for many years. I asked him to tell me something about him.

"Well, his father—who set up the company, by the way—is a decorated veteran of the Winter War. One of the Finnish Civic Guard ski-troop commanders who survived Suomussalmi."

"What was that? Sounds like food poisoning!"

"It was a very famous battle—Second World War. And I wouldn't joke about it if I were you. Matti, I should tell you, is very proud of his father. And, by the way, his wife—the beautiful Marjo—is a well-known investigative journalist with Finnish national television."

"Oh!"

"That's exactly what I said when I first saw her. Are you interested or not in this prime prospective client?"

"Very! Send him to me forthwith, my good man."

Matti Kovero arrived two weeks later. He was tall, bespectacled, and serious but not humourless, which was just as well, because "full-immersion" courses can be very wearing.

One morning, during one of our frequent breaks, we were standing out on our front steps, gazing out over the countryside and enjoying the bleak sunshine.

"Tapio tells me you have frequent bouts of journalism," he remarked, employing a Tapio-like quirky sense of humour and newly acquired idiomatic phrase.

"Not frequent enough," I sighed, "but I'm working on something at the moment."

"Is it interesting?"

I told him about Arthur Kass.

"From Estonia?" he asked in astonishment. "Here, in this little town?"

I could understand his reaction. It was 1985—five years before the Berlin Wall came down and before the break-up of the USSR in 1991. No one was talking about Gorbachev, glasnost, or Perestroika.

"Would you like to meet him?" I asked. "I was hoping to see him this afternoon."

"I'd love to!"

He seemed preoccupied and excited. I said nothing, waiting for him to explain.

"My wife, as you know, works for Finnish television. She made her name researching Estonia's part in the Second World War."

Kass's wife Alma ushered us into the living room. It was all done in a constrained silence. We stood stiffly and waited. Logs spat energetically in the great stone fireplace at the end of the room.

Arthur Kass had his back to us, slowly levering himself up out of an armchair. His eyes flickered over me but came to rest on Matti.

Kass knew why I had come, but he said, "Is the clock going all right for you?"

"Yes, perfectly. This is Mr Matti Kovero from Finland."

"From Finland?"

Matti stepped forward in brisk, military fashion, hand extended. With an old-fashioned little bow and click of the heels, he rattled off something in Finnish. Arthur responded in similar fashion and with surprising energy. What he said could have been Finnish or Estonian—at that stage, they sounded much the same to me. Later, I was given to understand that Finns and Estonians can easily communicate, because the languages are closely related.

Kass's stone-hewn features had become animated. He turned and said something to his wife. She became animated because he was.

"Why don't we all sit down," said Kass, without looking at me. Suddenly, I had become marginalized.

There was silence as we settled into four rickety armchairs.

Outside, tall poplars and birches sighed in the wind. Out on the river, wild geese called raucously. There was splashing and a beating of wings as unseen birds took off.

Arthur Kass turned to me. Courteously he said, "Please excuse us, but this is very, very interesting for us."

"It's okay," I said. "Go ahead."

The wife gave me a grateful smile. It was clear that I could have offered to come back later, but it would have disrupted the intense, emotional mood that prevailed. It had come about suddenly, and I could only guess why.

Two hours later, in the car, I said to Matti, "So, Matti, what was all that about?"

He was still on a high, like someone who had seen a really inspiring film. Slowly he turned to me, eyes lit up, slightly flushed.

"It's one of the great so-called coincidences of life," he said, almost reverently.

I looked at him, waiting for him to go on.

"He knew my father!" he said. "Before the Winter War."

"Where was this?" I asked casually, concentrating on avoiding a cyclist with no luminous armband. It was getting dark.

When Matti looked at me again, the light had left his eyes. I was a stranger, an outsider, who has not taken part, who did not appreciate the magic of his father's past.

"In Finland," he said coldly and looked away.

We were silent all the way back to the house.

I decided to call Tapio.

"How's Matti?" was the first thing he wanted to know. I told him, and he laughed.

"Tapio, I need some serious background here."

"Concerning what?"

"You know, Finland-Estonia, the Winter War. Matti's hero father . . ."

"What do you need that for, specifically?"

I told him about Arthur Kass knowing Matti's father. He was suitably impressed.

"Right. It's December 1939. Finland is being attacked by Russia. There's 700 miles of border to defend—from southern Finland to the Arctic. We had 100,000 Finnish Civic Guard to patrol it. Advancing towards us in a twenty-mile-long column are 500,000 Russian troops with tanks, planes, heavy guns. You know what the Finnish Civic Guard had against that lot?"

"What?"

"Machine pistols, 70,000 home-made Molotov cocktails, and sticks of dynamite—"

"Where do the Estonians come in?"

"Right. Estonia is still at peace. They weren't invaded for another six months. Every December and January, the sea at the eastern end of the gulf between Finland and Estonia freezes over. All through December 1939, Estonian volunteers were crossing the ice to join the Finnish Civic Guard. Russian planes strafed them by day. Russian sleigh patrols came at them like wolf packs by night. Kass was more than likely involved in that—"

"Okay. What was this Suo . . . Suo—"

"Suomussalmi. Place on the border. Central Finland. That's where the biggest battle of the Winter War took place—29 December. It was an incredible victory for the Finns, and Matti's father was one of the heroes. He was some kind of section commander."

"How did Arthur Kass meet your father?" I asked at coffee break next morning.

"Did Tapio tell you anything about the Winter War?"

"He did, very briefly—your father's role, the Estonians crossing the ice, all that . . ."

He nodded dryly, still displeased with me. I wanted self-service, and his past was a feast.

"It was 27 December 1939—two days before the Battle of Suomussalmi. Arthur Kass arrived with a group of Estonian veterans at the section of the front commanded by my father—"

"Veterans?"

"Kass's group had crossed the ice and fought in Finland before. On this occasion, they'd been badly shot up by Russian sleigh patrols crossing the ice. Kass's great friend Toivo had been torn to pieces by Russian gunfire before his eyes. He regrouped his men and wiped out the three Russian patrols. He arrived in my father's camp with badly needed Russian guns and ammunition. He demanded and was given command of his own veterans on the front at Suomussalmi. His men became one of the crack units of ski troops which turned the tide at Suomussalmi."

Now it was my turn to be thoughtful. What Matti had said threw a completely new light on the story of Arthur Kass.

I found Matti gazing at me, his funny little smile in place. His eyes glinted behind his glasses, still with a touch of permafrost.

"So now," he said, "what is it you'd *really* like to know?"

I looked at him. There was a preliminary question to be answered first.

"Was this group of Estonian veterans—Kass's men—the nucleus of the resistance that came into being later in Estonia?"

"That's exactly right!"

He waited happily to field my next question.

"Okay. So that means that—so far as you are concerned—Arthur Kass's story about leading the Estonian Resistance is true?"

He went on looking at me. The tight little smile had slowly drained out of his face.

"Of course it was—and *is*—true!"

It was said almost in a whisper, but there could be no mistaking the contempt and vehemence in that voice. He went on staring at me in disbelief. At that moment, I didn't care—I'd got a handle on the story of Arthur Kass. Things started to move quickly after that.

About two weeks later, I went down to see the Kass couple in response to a phone call. I found them in a jubilant mood, wanting to pour me some home-made wine in celebration.

"What's it all about?" I asked.

"Matti's wife," Arthur announced, "phoned me today from Finland—"

"To make the story on TV in Finland!" said Alma.

"I have some good news myself!" I announced. "The London publisher Marjo contacted is definitely interested!"

I had rewritten two chapters and a synopsis, at Arthur's request, and sent them off.

"This is marvellous!" said Arthur. "Now we *must* have a drink!"

So saying, he got the neck of the bottle firmly onto the glass beside me. But it rattled, and I could see that his hand shook. I looked at him. This was a man nearing eighty years of age. He still had fine, clear-cut features, white hair, and grey-blue eyes like chips off an iceberg. He had the erect spine and bearing of a soldier used to command. He was also pale and ill-looking. I knew that he had survived two heart attacks and a bypass operation. I felt nothing but admiration for him.

After a couple of glasses, Alma became positively playful.

"Jumal!" she exclaimed to me. "Mein 'usband is going to be interview on Finland national TV!"

I nodded enthusiastically whilst dealing with a mouthful of wine.

"Mooshi!" she called playfully to her husband. "Now you must cut your hair!" To me, she said, "He is looking like a pop star from TV!"

"Yes, he is, isn't he?"

Arthur had an announcement to make. He lifted a forefinger to emphasize its importance.

"Today . . . I make my first excursion to the new his-&-hers hair-cutting salon!"

Alma rose in mock protest, "No! I not have those women feasting on you with their hungry eyes! I going to get the scissors *now*! I do myself!"

As she flounced past him towards the kitchen, he applied a surprisingly quick slap to her ample rump, eliciting an almost girlish shriek. I could easily imagine a flaunting, possessive young Alma.

We heard her rattling things noisily in a kitchen drawer.

"Mooshi!" she wailed. "I cannot find it!"

"Never mind!" he called back. "We do it later."

We listened as she rummaged some more.

Finally, she called, "I go out in the garden now. Tell if you want coffee!"

We heard her close the back door and then the clump of boots, fading away.

"It's not really good news from the publisher, is it?"

I found Arthur looking at me sharply.

"I'm afraid not. The publisher seems to want conclusive proof."

He nodded reflectively.

"Marjo wants the same thing."

"You mean proof? Is that a problem?"

"She wants to interview not only me but former comrades as well. It amounts to the same thing."

"Which comrades have survived?"

He glanced sharply at me and then hung his head reflectively without answering. I had encountered the same reluctance each time I'd broached the subject before, but now I had to know. At the same time, I was listening to Alma quietly replacing the latch on the back door. She must have stood there, listening, and Arthur knew she was there.

With a sigh, he said, "Peeter Sirel and Aarand Tofer have survived. They're the only ones now who—"

Alma came striding into the room and said forcefully, "Never I let two such men sit in TV interview with Arthur! After everything we live through in the War! After everything our friends, relations, and family die for! Never these two men! One is criminal! Other is . . . crazy person, alcoholic, depressed man!"

Her indignation seemed to choke off whatever else she wanted to say. She scooped up a bundle of washing and swept from the room. I looked to Arthur for an explanation. He was rolling the makings of a cigarette between his fingers, giving himself time to think.

When he'd released the first big intake of smoke he said, "Towards the end of the War, Sirel went a bit crazy . . ."

"But he was your second in command—"

"Not at the end, he wasn't! Johann Semmal was."

"What happened to Semmal?"

"Killed in Viljandi Forest, 1956, leading the last of the men we left behind."

"What about Tofer?"

"He runs a ski school in Austria. He's changed his name."

"What kind of man is he?"

"You've read the manuscript. He was and is a rough-house sergeant. A killer."

I had a visual image of Tofer and his mate Corporal Eduard Poom. They were into everything from black marketeering to currency dealing—with the Germans, with the Russians, with anybody. Did Arthur just turn a blind eye to it?

"He was practically a criminal!" I said.

"They *were* criminals—both of them!"

Things began falling into place. I could certainly see why Tofer should not speak for Arthur and the resistance on Finnish TV.

"What about Sirel?"

"Sirel . . . was brilliant. He set up, trained, and himself led three small commando units for use behind enemy lines. We used Sirel's units as the blueprint for converting our entire force of partisans into advance units for German Army Group North when we went into Russia in 1941."

I could see it all as he spoke. Night raids, ski patrols, arms dumps exploding in the crimson night. The chatter of Schmeissers, the crack of Degtyarevs, knifings, sudden death . . .

"You're saying Sirel changed in some way?"

"Yes. The tide of the War turned. Our German allies were in retreat from the Russian Front. We realized that they were trying to use us as a buffer between them and the advancing Russian Army. Among our men, it created a tremendous feeling of two-time betrayal, disillusion, and bitterness. Discipline came close to collapsing. We shot some of our own men for crimes like rape, looting, arson . . . Sirel became a complete fanatic, shooting men point-blank with a handgun. He was cracking up."

He stopped to lean forward slowly. He took the poker and moved a log into the hot centre of the fire. He looked like a sick old man.

"So," I said at length, "what happened?"

"We escaped to Sweden—about 500 men. We were interned for what remained of the War."

He paused as if to try to remember what happened next.

"In the internment camp, Corporal Eduard Poom was found strangled one morning. He'd been tortured beforehand. Sirel was arrested and tried but acquitted for lack of sufficient evidence."

"Were you involved in the proceedings?"

"Yes. The authorities acknowledged me as leader of the internees."

"Was Sirel guilty?"

"Does it matter?"

We were silent for quite a while after that, both gazing into the fire. I wasn't satisfied with the way Arthur's account had concluded.

"Arthur, what is it you're not telling me about Sirel?"

He looked at me sharply and fixed me with a long, considering gaze. At length, he said, "I never trusted Sirel."

"Why?"

"From the very beginning, he was working for German intelligence."

Now it was my turn to give Arthur Kass a good long look. I felt a door was being opened, because there were things in his manuscript which went unexplained.

"Where did Sirel acquire the expertise to set up three commando units of the kind you describe? He was a journalist before the War."

He released a big lungful of smoke and picked a piece of loose tobacco off his tongue before replying.

"If I knew then what I know now, that book might have been different."

He indicated the pile of manuscript on the table with a movement of his chin.

"Different in what way?"

"In summer 1940, after the defeat of the British and French, Finland came under threat from Russia. Marshal Mannerheim of Finland looked to Germany for protection. A secret SS battalion was formed in Finland. It was part of the Fifth SS-Panzergrenadierdivision 'Wiking.' After the deportation of the Estonian government in June 1940, Sirel disappeared to Finland and joined up."

"What's the connection with German Intelligence?"

"He was clearly recruited during his SS training in Finland."

"Do you know anyone who could confirm this?"

Alma had come back into the room very quietly. I had a feeling she'd been listening in. She and Arthur exchanged a few words in low, serious tones. Then they both turned and gazed seriously at me.

"I have a German friend who could confirm it."

"Could you put me in direct contact with Peeter Sirel?"

Arthur and Alma exchanged serious glances.

"I haven't spoken to Peeter Sirel in over thirty years."

"Can you contact him?"

"Yes, I can. Let me think about it. Can you come back, say, tomorrow afternoon?"

When I called the following afternoon, I found them both subdued and upset. Arthur in particular was pale and ill-looking. I thought it wiser to wait for an explanation.

At length, Arthur said, "I spoke to Sirel this morning."

Alma was staring hard at me.

"Mein 'usband now sick again. Is heart. Doctor come soon, so . . ."

I looked at Arthur. He merely nodded. It was clearly not a moment to pursue the matter.

Shortly after this, Arthur Kass became seriously ill for the first time and was in and out of hospital until his death later that year.

⌒⚭⚭⌒

One night in June, I drove down to the little harbour and parked on the edge of the quay, high above the water. A rich, three-quarters moon hung in a dark-blue sky. Boats rocked gently against the quay wall.

I knew Arthur was home from the hospital, convalescing. I hadn't phoned, because Alma always answered, and she seemed to want to keep me at bay for the sake of Arthur's health—hence my intended surprise visit.

It was only when I switched off the engine that I became aware of the rich, pulsating music wafting over the night air. Through the dense foliage of the birches, I saw the lights full on in the Kasses' house, the windows thrown open. Inside, two figures swept back and forth, swirling in time to the dance music, arms locked around each other like two young lovers, ghosts from the big-band era. Arthur said something, his voice strong but low. Alma threw back her head and laughed in that hoarse, abandoned way she had.

Immediately, I saw a picture of Arthur and Alma in the Du Nord Club on a night in the spring of 1940. It was during that strange, six-month period between Arthur's return from the Winter War in Finland and the invasion of Estonia by the Russians in June. It was the period when Tallinn seethed with communist agitators, Soviet and German spies, and Nazi activists. The Du Nord was a microcosm of that world. Every conceivable representative of those different forces seemed to be there on that night, 17 April, the night they celebrated Alma's birthday, when he intended to announce their engagement.

It had been a mere twenty years since Estonia's independence from Russia. In that period, Estonia had developed exponentially in the fields of industry, commerce, farming, and shipbuilding. He, Arthur Kass, successful timber exporter, who mixed with the best society in the Baltic sailing fraternity, was about to marry Alma, daughter of one of the new shipping tycoons.

Arthur Kass loved life, loved his country, and most of all at that moment, he loved Alma. Yet as he steered her round the dance floor, he could see everywhere in the shadowed recesses of the club that night men who seemed bent on destroying everything he believed in.

There, at a table in one of the arched recesses, was Helmuth Metsas, future leader of the puppet government under the Nazis in 1941. Much more sinister was his drinking companion, Alfons Rebane, the rabid SS division commander who would send so many Russians and Jews to a shameful death at Vaivara concentration camp.

In another recess, a group everyone studiously ignored—Estonian Communist Party leader Anton Kepman, recently released from jail, arrogantly loud among his cronies. More dangerous by far was the man beside him—Andrei Ivanovitch Zdanov, head of the trade delegation at the Russian Embassy. Few realized until later that it was he who spun out the web of intrigue from the embassy which resulted in what TASS called "the spontaneous uprising of the working people" against the legitimately elected government of

Estonia. It was this fabrication which was to be the excuse for the Russian invasion of Estonia in June 1940.

Over in the corner, a head taller than the group surrounding him, stood Sasha Veinberg, resplendent in evening dress, smoking a cigarette in a long amber holder. The apparently effete scion of the fabulously wealthy Veinbergs was a sincere socialist, something that was possible in a country where the German Baltic barons were still the kings of industry and commerce, and the distribution of wealth was a controversial issue. The communists sneered at him, and many refused to take him seriously. If only Arthur had understood what a role Sasha was to play in all of their lives.

This group, in turn, studiously avoided another man society seemed to disapprove of—Peeter Sirel, ensconced in another recess with a darkly beautiful woman. A candle on the table between them illuminated their faces, bent towards each other in earnest conversation. This was Kaisa Jarvinen, a Finnish journalist. It was only later that Arthur Kass discovered that she was also part of the Finnish intelligence service. If only Arthur Kass had understood his former comrade from their Winter War days in Finland . . .

Two government ministers stood on the edge of Sasha's group, fielding questions. One was idealistic and naive, the other smug and overconfident. Noticeable by their absence that night were the conniving, self-seeking, cynical, or ruthless ones. But it didn't matter, because Estonian politicians collectively and individually had in their own ways, at that crucial moment in history, failed their people by lulling them into a false sense of security. The Mutual Assistance Pact, signed with the USSR in 1939 and internationally ratified, would guarantee all their futures. Arthur Kass and his former comrades had no such illusions.

Very few people in Estonia at that moment knew of the secret Molotov-Ribbentrop Pact which placed Estonia firmly in Stalin's "sphere of influence." One of the few was Zdanov, secretly appointed head of the NKVD in Estonia, mandated to prepare the ground for the coming invasion.

I heard a deep growl from within as their Great Dane sensed my presence. The dancers halted. The music was turned down, and Arthur came to the window. I had started the car by then and was moving off.

I had one crucial meeting with him before his death.

⌀ຕ໙

Chapter 2

IT WASN'T UNTIL 10 December that I managed to see Arthur Kass alone, when he was back in hospital once again. I asked him how he was. He made a barely perceptible movement, like a corpse stirring. It clearly said, "You see how I am!"

We lapsed into silence, thinking our own thoughts.

"Your German," he gasped, "is good enough to interview Tofer—"

"Arthur—"

"You must want to meet them, Sirel and Tofer?"

"The publishers in London would insist on it, yes."

"Marjo has in fact set up the interview for 5 January." He paused. "I know I'm dying. I won't be here to meet her."

I was shocked.

"Do you want to do this for us?" he asked very quietly.

"Yes!" I heard myself saying. My voice was hoarse.

"Start with Tofer! I'll have to phone him first—won't talk to you otherwise."

"Arthur—"

"I can't do it today. Tomorrow! Can you come?"

"Yes!"

"Come in the morning!" he commanded.

Arthur was in a sitting position with pillows at his back. The bed had been moved close to the door. There was a trolley against it, on which there was a black telephone handset with a lead extending out into the corridor. Considering his condition, I could only marvel at how quickly he had arranged everything.

I dialled the number in Austria, and a woman answered. It was pure Hochdeutsch in a beautifully modulated voice.

"Yes," she said. "He's somewhere around. I'll just go and fetch him."

The next voice was a man's.

"Yes?" he growled suspiciously.

"Herr Kastner?" Tofer too had changed his name.

"Yes!"

"I have a call for you. Just a moment."

I handed the phone to Arthur. He paused for a moment before speaking.

"Aarand?" he began. The rest was a babble of Estonian. At the beginning, he seemed to be explaining. He ended with what sounded like instructions.

"Tofer will see you any time. This week, if you like—"

"What about Sirel?"

Arthur became quite still, staring intently at the wall behind me, the eyes blinking at intervals. The effort to decide something was almost tangible.

"I understand he's in quite a big way of business now."

"Where is he?"

"London." The voice was hoarse, almost a gasp.

At this point, the ward door was abruptly flung open. A young nurse backed in, negotiating a loaded trolley through. Without preamble, she commenced to noisily pull the curtains around Arthur's bed.

Ignoring me, she said brightly, "How are we this morning, Mr Kass?"

Without waiting for a reply, she said to me, "Sorry, sir, visiting hours are over now."

"What about Sirel?" I asked Arthur.

He was still gazing at the wall as if the nurse wasn't there.

"He's an arms dealer!"

"How can I contact him?"

The nurse heaved a big sigh and stood waiting, hand on hip. Arthur turned his head slowly to look at me.

"Alma has the number," he whispered.

I nodded and made to move.

"Can you bring Alma to the hospital tonight?" he said faintly.

"Yes, of course!"

Arthur Kass died at 4.00 a.m. the following morning.

At the funeral, I was preoccupied with the fact that Alma's attitude towards me had changed. Now I seemed to be viewed as an importunate writer, from whose intrusion she felt obliged to retreat further into the mystery of their past. This both puzzled and saddened me. Did they have something to hide? Had I but known it, the answer to that conundrum could have been found much sooner in the composition of the group of well-dressed strangers who attended the proceedings. I wished later that I had paid more attention to them. It wasn't fated to happen like that.

After the funeral, I went down to see Alma. We talked in desultory fashion for a while and then lapsed into silence. Suddenly she stirred, fixed me with a look as Arthur used to do, and said, "You come for Sirel's phone number?"

"Yes!"

"I get."

She returned in a few minutes and placed a crumpled, grubby envelope in front of me. A number had been scrawled on it in biro.

"Today, I like visit Arthur's grave," she announced. Her voice was, if anything, deeper and hoarser.

"I'll take you!"

"Thank you!"

The graveyard was deserted, dusted with snow. I stayed in the car, listening to the wind moaning through the crosses. Crows squabbled in a tree, two fields away.

Alma had brought something to kneel on. For a long time she stayed there, seemingly oblivious of the cold or her surroundings. Then I saw her begin to rock back and forth, her face contorted, with a sort of moaning or sobbing sound. There was something primeval about it, which sent a chill through me. Immediately, I had a vision of Tallinn, 5 January 1940, six months before the Russian invasion.

Towards sunset that day, as the skyline of spires and towers went black against the reddening sky, Alma restlessly awaited Arthur's return from Finland. With surreal normality, an army brass band was playing up in the wooden pavilion, above the frozen Snelli Tiik, across which skaters glided and called out gaily to each other. As darkness fell, floodlights were switched on, and steam could be seen rising in clouds from the hot-drinks stands, and still he didn't come. The distant boom of the Russian guns, up at the Mannerheim Line, echoed the brass percussion from across the frozen gulf. From inside the Du Nord Club, where she waited, they were bizarre sounds from an unhinged world. For all she knew, Arthur could have been lying out there, dead on the ice. Then he appeared, a white-faced ghost, in the doorway, and at once she was in his arms, sobbing and holding him, never wanting to let him go again.

When we drew up at Alma's house, she made no attempt to get out. She went on staring through the windscreen.

"He was *good* man, Aleks!" she said forcefully, her voice almost a croak. "Best I ever meet!"

She turned and fixed me with one of those looks.

"Never that you forget!" she instructed me fiercely. With that, she got out.

Within two months, Alma was dead. She never showed any sign of illness. She just went as if she had lost the will to live.

A solicitor phoned me one day, in connection with the disposal of the Kass's property, which included Arthur's manuscript. I told him that I had it and that it could be collected at his firm's convenience. They never called for it, and I still have it.

At the time, I took this turn of events as an indication that Alma did not, after all, wish to have the story published. With deep regret, I ceased all efforts in that connection. There seemed to be no point then in contacting Sirel or Tofer. It appeared to be such a futile and meaningless ending. But it was not the end. In fact, it was only the beginning.

⚬〰〰〰⚬

Five years passed. On 19 January 1991, an incident occurred which unexpectedly brought the Kass story back to life. A man shot himself dead while his wife was in the town shopping. It had happened on an island in the lake. I knew the couple. They were German.

The following morning, I was intrigued to see a Garda squad car coming in through our gates. A tall, military figure with iron-grey hair and moustache got out. It was Martin Cusack, a Garda detective I knew quite well. I was immediately aware of an uncharacteristic intensity in his manner.

"Is there somewhere we can have a private chat?"

"Sure! We can go in the kitchen."

As soon as we were seated, he said, "You heard about the German who shot himself?"

"I've just heard! Hans Kersting, he's called."

There was a pause while he considered me.

"John, those trips you were making out to the Germans last winter. Can you tell me what that was all about?"

"Okay. Harry Kennedy took me out to see them, because he wanted me to take over what he was doing. He's not getting any younger . . ."

I was reluctant to go on.

"What *was* he doing?"

"He was taking out food and firewood—to the wife."

"You mean, giving it to them?"

"They had no money left, Martin. Banks wouldn't let them sign any more cheques."

"You mean while Hans was still driving round in that big white BMW?"

"Harry went on giving him credit for petrol—"

"Did Hans think he could turn things round or what?"

"He certainly went on trying. The banks didn't want to know. He was on the point of losing that car at any moment."

"You think . . . was it because of the situation that he killed himself?"

I immediately sensed something underlying the question.

"Unless you have information that says otherwise, Martin."

He glanced towards the door.

"This is strictly off the record."

I nodded.

"Hans made an illegal transfer of money to an account in Germany. There may be other transfers. The banks have got court orders to seize his assets."

"God!"

"So you know them well? *Knew* them?"

"Yes."

"Would you come with me, to help me talk to her?"

"I don't think that would be a good idea, Martin," I said rather coldly.

He stared at me, quite unabashed.

"They may be other factors you are unaware of."

"What other factors?"

"The Gardai in fact had already taken an interest in the German's story."

"Why was that?"

"Well, for example, among other things, he received a phone call last week from the Israeli Embassy in London."

"How could the Gardai know that, Martin, unless they were tapping his phone?"

"Look, we're getting into deep water here, John—"

"Is this an official Garda investigation?"

"Why do you ask?"

"These people are friends of mine!"

"We're not doing anything official here, John. We're just having a chat."

"Why not make a simple enquiry at the Israeli Embassy?"

"Our instructions are to find out all we can at this end first."

"One thing I can tell you, Martin, is that Hans was no Nazi exterminator or whatever it is the Gardai imagine—"

"The fact is, John, that we don't know what was going on, do we?" We looked hard at each other.

"I think, in fact," I said at length, "that I would like to go out there with you and see what's happening. But I can't promise anything!"

"That's fair enough," he said. He looked relieved, I thought.

The roar of the boat's engine started a frantic flapping of wildlife and bore into the vast silence of the lake. Gradually coming into focus were the dark-blue uniforms of the local Gardaí—quite a few of them—watching our approach from the island's harbour.

The local sergeant greeted us with "How are the men?" and watched as we tied up.

His manner was dry and distant.

"This man is with me," said Martin as soon as we stood on land. He spoke with quiet authority.

"They're interviewing the wife at the moment, so—"

"Right!" said Martin decisively. "We'll wait over there." We walked off towards the house.

The house was a wooden structure with a veranda, on a slight rise, in a clearing among the trees. The setting was idyllic. We sat on a great flat rock and watched the muted drama being enacted behind a large picture window.

Hilge Kersting sat in an armchair facing us, flanked by two men. The one who sat on a couch to her left had darkish skin, thick white hair, and a heavy moustache. He spoke only occasionally in a deep, quiet voice. It was clear that he was a foreigner.

The other was a large man, in what looked like an expensive suit. He moved restlessly about the room and fired questions in a loud, hectoring tone. From his manner, I guessed he was the senior Garda officer present.

"That's Tom Hessian," said Martin dryly.

"Who's the other man?"

"Don't know."

I could hear Hilge replying in that calm, even tone I knew so well. She spoke English perfectly but with a slight accent. There was a touch of Marlene Dietrich about her. It was a beautiful, musical voice.

A group of Gardaí emerged from the back of the house, accompanied by a bearded man wearing a white hooded coat and white wellingtons. A trolley, bearing Hans's body in a body bag, was wheeled around the corner, silently past us, and down to the harbour. The stretcher was lowered onto one of the boats which chugged slowly out into the lake.

The drama behind the window continued. Suddenly it was over, and the big man exited with the same violent energy. Martin Cusack stood up to intercept him.

"Well, Tom, what's the story?"

"You'll be told in good time!" he threw back, and he was gone.

A sergeant stopped and said, "Martin, this is Mr Habermel, from Israel."

The handsome, stocky man with the white hair and moustache was beautifully dressed in a tan-coloured suit and fawn overcoat.

"Pleasure!" he said and shook the detective's hand. He had gold caps on two front teeth.

"I must catch the boat," he said, pointing to it, and he was away off down the path.

Suddenly, all the remaining Gardaí were moving down towards the boats.

"Waste of time trying to interview her now," said Martin Cusack.

"Look, I'll stay and talk to her, okay?"

He nodded and walked away.

I knew she would hear my footsteps on the wooden floor of the veranda. I knocked gently on the screen door.

"Yes!" called the voice firmly from inside.

I walked in. She hadn't moved from the armchair, and she watched me approach.

"John!" she said faintly.

I knelt down and took her hand. It was limp and damp.

"You okay?"

She nodded, still in shock.

"I'll get you some tea."

"Thank you."

I went into the kitchen and started getting the tea things ready.

The drone of the engines was already fading. Bird calls were restored to the background sounds, and the singing of the kettle filled the kitchen. I put some bread in the toaster and then found Hans's whiskey bottle on a shelf above the wellingtons.

I walked in without saying anything, set up a little folding table in front of her, and then went to fetch the tray.

"I want you to take this glass and swallow the whole thing in one go. Like this!"

She gazed at the whiskey, lifted it, and then swallowed it as instructed, leaving the glass down with a gasp. It shocked her into life.

"Take the tea now and that bit of cheese and toast. I'm going to clean up inside."

I padded around the kitchen for a while, doing this and that, keeping an eye on her surreptitiously. She slowly got through everything on the tray, and then I heard the scratch of a match. There was a whiff of sulphur and fresh cigarette smoke. I came back in.

"Would you like me to sit with you for a while?"

She nodded and moved to the couch, and I sat down beside her. She took my hand.

"Thank you for coming! I'm not able to talk about anything yet."

"That's all right! We'll just sit here together for a while."

We sat like that for a long time. I could hear the clock on the wall behind, but I didn't want to turn around for fear of disturbing her. She had fallen into a deep sleep and then came to with a start.

"Maybe I should go now?"

"Don't go just yet."

She lit another cigarette, inhaling deeply, as if monitoring the internal effects.

"I haven't stopped thinking about Nadja and Aleks, you know, these past few months."

"I'm not sure I . . . ?"

"Nadja. I still think of her as Nadja Semmal—"

"Semmal? There was a Johann Semmal, who was Aleks's—"

"Yes. Nadja was Johann Semmal's sister."

Instantly, I saw the lake in Viljandi, Estonia, 1956, and the figure of Johann running towards it, and then Russian paratroopers coming out of the trees, automatic weapons stuttering. And Johann is jerking and spinning, his body shredding, and the startled birds rising in flocks off the water behind.

"Nadja and Aleks, you said?"

"Yes, Nadja and Aleks. Or Alma and Arthur Kass, as you call them."

"Alma was Nadja Semmal, Johann's sister?"

I felt strangely disturbed. The whole Kass story was being disinterred.

"Yes. Are you all right, John?"

"Yes, it's just that—"

"Yes, I know—all the secrecy and subterfuge. If you'd lived through the War and the Stalinist era in Estonia as we did, I think you'd understand."

I stared at her.

"But I understood you were German. Is that not correct?"

"It is, and it isn't. I was brought up in a German-speaking community in Estonia. I'm Jewish, in fact. Sasha Veinberg was my older brother."

Sasha Veinberg! I could scarcely believe what I was hearing.

"So, in fact, you've known Arthur—Aleks and Nadja—a long time?"

She slowly exhaled a deep intake of smoke, looking into the past.

"I've loved Aleks—all my life—since I was a girl of seventeen."

She gazed at me calmly. I envisioned how, earlier, I had seen the Gardaí wheeling Hans's body down to the boat in the bleak sunshine.

"Did Nadja know?"

It elicited a small, grim smile. She looked out at the lake or the distance.

"Oh, she knew all right, because I told her."

"What was her reaction?"

She took her time, making a ceremony of stubbing out the cigarette.

"Nadja was a very special person. She showed me nothing but compassion. Even when I told her how I tried to betray her."

"Betray in what way?"

"I mean *betray*. Betray her to the secret police—the NKVD."

There was something tremendously intense in her, accentuated by her calm, low-key delivery and the pallor of her face.

"I never knew anything about this side of the story, Hilge."

"You can have no idea of the kind of person I was then. I was experiencing an incredibly intense, jealous passion for a man twice my age. I was only seventeen."

Looking at her then, I thought in fact that I did have some idea.

"You know what I did?"

I shook my head.

"I made up my mind that I would meet Aleks alone in his flat, up near the Viru Gate, in the old quarter."

"When was this?"

"I could never forget that date. It was 25 June 1940, exactly five days after the NKVD had deported the Estonian government to Russia, from the Baltic Station."

Immediately, I could see the young Russian soldiers strolling through the streets, the Estonian Regular Army brass band still playing up on the little wooden pavilion, above the waters of the Snelli Tiik, people eating ice cream under striped awnings, outside cafés along the Viru Valjak, in out of the hot sun.

"Did you know Aleks was the leader of the resistance?"

"I knew nothing! Nothing but passion! The concierge told me that Aleks was out. But I sneaked up the stairs, up onto the roof garden."

She paused in sudden deep thought.

"What happened?"

She smiled her grim little smile.

"It was a very warm, sunny afternoon. I fell asleep behind a big chimney, up on the flat roof. I woke up hours later when I heard someone come into Aleks's flat. I was about to knock on his window when someone threw it wide open with a big laugh and called out something to Aleks in the room behind. A woman's voice—Nadja's."

She stopped, staring into the distance across the lake, her eyes blank with the film of past events.

"I'll never forget the next few hours. I crouched behind the chimney, beside the open window, listening to the sounds of their lovemaking inside. I was wearing only a thin blouse. I must have been frozen, but I remember nothing of that."

Long, slow sunsets turn the rooftops and chimneys and spires of Tallinn into black silhouettes, the streets below into shadowed canyons, echoing passing feet and hollow laughter.

"How did you betray her?"

"Hours later, they started talking seriously about things I'd never imagined—sabotage, derailment of trains. They were speaking in Estonian. I could hear every word."

"Why in Estonian?"

"Nadja and Johann belonged to the Russian-speaking Estonian minority. Her first language was Russian."

She smiled a self-deprecating smile, as if still embarrassed by some memory.

"I was terrified of the NKVD. Everyone was. I wanted to betray Nadja, but I was afraid and didn't know how to go about it. Then I thought of my brother Sasha."

"Did you know Sasha was in the resistance?"

"I had no idea! I just knew that he was a senior civil servant, with responsibility for state security, or the police, or something like that. Anyway, he was important."

"So you went to Sasha, to report overhearing—"

"I went to Sasha's office. I blurted out everything, changing a few details, of course. You know what he did?"

I shook my head.

"This was in police headquarters. He took me into an empty office, sat me down, and carefully explained how dangerous it was to have anything to do with the NKVD. They made informers go back to spy. They never let them off the hook and so on. In short, he terrified the life out of me—in his subtle way—and told me to leave everything to him. After that, it was as if Nadja and Aleks had disappeared off the face of the earth. I didn't see them again until many years later."

There was a splashing and flapping of wings outside and the distant honking of Siberian geese echoed down the lake. Dusk wasn't far off.

"How did Hans come into your life?"

Suddenly, she sat up straight, taking a deep breath. Hans was a different story. She seemed to be marshalling the facts in her head.

"Before the Russians took over in Estonia, Hitler had made an agreement with Stalin called the Molotov-Ribbentrop Pact. One of the terms of this pact was that German-speaking Estonians would be repatriated to Germany. Hans came to Estonia as a member of the commission set up to carry out this task."

"So he was a civil servant too?"

"No, he was a regular army officer—Wehrmacht, seconded to the commission. I can't remember why."

"So?"

"Well, Sasha, my brother, was appointed to the same commission as liaison officer, representing the interests of Estonian—in fact Russian—state security."

"That's rather ironic, isn't it?"

"Yes. The Germans had lots of money. They organized social functions, threw parties. I got invited to one—"

"And that's how you met Hans?"

"Yes, that's how I met Hans."

She looked down, suddenly sad, at the backs of her hands placed formally on her lap, as if contemplating the ring on the fourth finger of her left hand.

"I didn't know it at the time, but Hans and Sasha were already involved in a secret and very dangerous enterprise together." She looked at me. "The German-speaking Jewish community was also to be 'repatriated' to Germany. An Estonian ship's captain was commissioned to take them there. He was instructed by Sasha and Hans to make a bolt for Sweden instead. He had been well paid to do so, because he could never return. I was on that ship."

She kept her gaze fixed intently on the backs of her hands, and there was something rigid in her posture.

"Why did Hans do it?"

Her eyes brimmed with tears, but her face remained impassive.

"He did it because he loved me. It was the bravest thing he ever did."

"What about Sasha?"

"I never saw my brother again. He stayed on in that office, until it was too late—altering files, destroying vital information, protecting Aleks, protecting everyone . . ."

"What happened to him?"

She was weeping openly and silently, but I knew she wanted to talk.

"One night in April 1941, Sasha was at the Baltic Station, watching a cattle train moving out, bearing thousands of his countrymen east to Siberia, when the NKVD arrived to arrest him. They bundled him into a car, and—"

Tears made two furrows down her face, dropping onto the blanket on her lap.

"Mr Habermel—who was here this morning—was on that ship too. Sasha told him to look after me in Sweden, and he did."

"What about Hans?"

"Hans, he found me in a DP camp in Sweden, after the War—through the Red Cross. We got married in Stockholm."

The red dusk was deepening. I wondered about switching on a lamp.

"Why did you never mention the connection with Aleks and Nadja when I was here with you all last winter?"

She came back from very far away and resettled herself on the couch.

"Well," she said with a deep sigh, "I didn't, for Hans' sake, really."

We looked at each other, both knowing that an explanation was in order.

"There's something, I think," she began, distilling her thoughts as she went along, "which has to be understood about men like Hans and Aleks. The War lifted then up like a tidal wave, carried them along like corks. Nothing was ever quite so real for them again. The War made them feel alive. Afterwards, they always lacked that real commitment, which is essential to make money in business."

"You think that was true of Aleks?"

"Yes," she said emphatically, "certainly it was! In Hans's case, there was another factor. He had a deep fear of poverty—a leftover from growing up in the Ruhrgebiet during the 1920s. Aleks was doing all right with his antique business. Hans's business was going down, down all the time. It created a kind of awkwardness between them. Poverty, even the fear of poverty, destroys everything. It destroys friendship. It takes the charm out of a man's personality. It destroys love."

We were silent for some time.

"As a result, I saw Nadja only once or twice during the last few years. The last time was the day she died."

We lapsed into silence again, thinking our own thoughts.

"And then suddenly, out of the blue, Mr Habermel turns up in Ireland?"

"Not out of the blue. He spent years trying to find out what had become of Sasha. Only last year, he traced us here to Ireland. Habermel had gone to Israel and has become rich. He's an exporter of citrus fruits."

"What did he want?"

"He wanted to find—and somehow thank—the two men who had saved his life by sending him to Sweden. He had formed an Estonian association in Israel for that purpose. As soon as they traced Hans here, they secured the agreement of the Israeli government to honour Hans publicly in some way."

"What's happened to that?"

"Then this business of Hans transferring money to Germany blew up. The police started investigating . . ."

Tears welled up suddenly in her eyes, and she choked back some strong emotion.

"He did it for me! Knowing he was going to end his life! He wanted me to be secure."

She shook her head at the irony of it.

"Last week, the Israeli Embassy in London phoned him to say that public honours were now not possible, considering the business with the police, and that Mr Habermel and his group were going to do something else for him."

Tears were streaming down her face.

"Hans really needed that positive gesture at that time, and suddenly, it was withdrawn."

"So the phone call from London was the last straw, as it were?"

"Something just snapped, and then—"

She wept openly, silently, and there wasn't a thing I could do but watch.

"Hilge," I said gently, "I don't understand why Mr Habermel was here today."

She started looking around her. I reached over, handing her the box of tissues. She dried her face, blew her nose, and suddenly seemed calm and composed again.

"Mr Habermel was in Dublin, arranging to set up a trust fund which would guarantee an income to Hans for the rest of his life."

"He must have been shocked out of his life when he heard about Hans."

"Yes. He drove down immediately. He's staying in Dublin for a few days more."

"What about the trust fund?"

"That's why he's staying in Dublin. He's arranging to have the terms changed so that the money can now be paid to me."

Suddenly, she was crying again, silently, her face contorted, not caring.

We were silent for a long time after she had calmed down, and we listened to the peaceful sounds in the gathering gloom. Then I took my leave.

However, even as the boat nosed out into the darkening mirror of the lake, questions were surfacing.

The following morning, I was approaching the island once more. There were two boats in the little harbour.

Hilge came out to greet me, and then the visitor came out and stood on the veranda beside her. It was Habermel. The casualness of his dress somehow suggested a certain intimacy between them. I had had no chance to see it, of course, the previous day. Suddenly, it struck me that they looked like a couple, much more than Hans and Hilge ever had. There was a certain proprietorial atmosphere between them. They turned and smiled at each other in sync, like two minds and hearts in harmony. It was like seeing two photographs that clashed—Hans in a body bag and this smiling couple. Which brought me to my first question: what was the full story concerning Habermel?

⊙⟩⟩⟩⟩⟩⟩⟩⟨⊙

Chapter 3

☙

THEY SAT TOGETHER on the couch. I sat in an armchair, facing them. I was aware of my own tension and of their relaxed postures.

"Hilge," I started, "I don't think you told me everything yesterday!"

They exchanged looks. Then she turned to me, the tiniest frown of concern between her brows.

"Everything I told you, John, was true."

"I'm certain of that myself. What I'm concerned about is what you did *not* tell me."

Habermel spoke for the first time. He had a deep, resonant voice.

"You came with a policeman! In the circumstances—"

"David," she remonstrated with him gently, putting her hand on top of his, "John is a friend. A good friend."

He nodded seriously in agreement and then remained silent, his liquid eyes going from one to the other of us as we spoke.

Hilge heaved a deep sigh as if wondering where to begin.

"My one regret in all this is that Hans may have died in vain."

Her voice quavered. Habermel immediately placed his hand on top of hers, looking concerned.

"You don't know what I'm talking about, do you?" she said with a regretful smile. I shook my head.

"It seems that—rather late in the day—I'm to inherit a substantial sum of money."

She extracted her hand from under Habermel's and rubbed the back of his, smiling warmly or gratefully. I was trying to come to terms with the unexpected turn the conversation had taken.

"Would it be indiscreet of me to enquire—"

"I have been given to understand that it is in the region of £4 m. sterling."

"And this money—"

"It has been lying in an account in Switzerland since early 1940."

"It was transferred there," said Habermel ponderously, "by Sasha Veinberg, Hilge's brother. Recovering this money has not been easy."

"Why?"

He looked to Hilge to provide the explanation.

"For nearly fifty years, Swiss banks and insurance companies have been demanding that the heirs of concentration camp victims produce death certificates to prove that the depositors were indeed dead. Before he put me on that ship to Sweden, my brother Sasha told me that he had persuaded my parents to put the money in the Swiss account in his name. In the event of his death, I was to inherit everything. He gave me all the relevant documents, which I still have."

"The problem was to produce his death certificate?"

"That's it exactly! We eventually discovered that Sasha had been taken to the Kazan psychiatric prison in Russia—"

She broke off and bit her lip. Habermel gripped her hand tightly.

"The TASS news agency," he continued, "reported that he had been put on trial and that he had confessed to 'crimes against the state.'"

She was weeping silently, her face strangely impassive.

"You know, of course, who Peeter Sirel is?" she said.

"Yes."

"And the name Zdanov?"

"Yes."

"Peeter is my half-brother. Zdanov is still a very powerful man in Russia today."

"Yes?"

"It proved impossible through official channels to get the death certificate we needed."

Habermel felt the need to intervene at this point.

"Peeter asked Zdanov to get it."

They exchanged significant looks.

"Did he demand a very high price or what?"

"Zdanov is a very dangerous man to do business with."

"At first," said Hilge, "he tried to get the money himself."

Habermel was nodding.

"Peeter has something Zdanov wants. It seems the situation can be negotiated."

They clearly didn't want to tell me more.

"Why do you think Aleks didn't want to put me in touch with your . . . with Peeter Sirel?"

They exchanged looks again. They seemed to be able to communicate without words. It had never been like that between Hans and Hilge. It was Habermel who answered.

"There were things Aleks did not mention in that manuscript of his, things he did not want mentioned, because he was ashamed of them."

I experienced a sinking feeling in my stomach.

"What exactly was he ashamed of?"

"The fact, for example, that the battalion he commanded, which fought in Russia in March 1943, was an SS battalion. This was the Twentieth Estonian SS Division. By June 1944, this division was assigned to the Third SS Korps, which was defending the Estonian border at Narva."

"Did Aleks do anything to be ashamed of?"

Again they exchanged looks. Now it seemed to be Hilge's turn to explain.

"John, Aleks was everything you think he was. He was honest, honourable, and very, very brave. He was a good man. He could also be stiff, proud, and puritanical. He did not want the image of his story to be tarnished or misunderstood."

Habermel was looking at me, nodding seriously.

"The Peeter Sirel he knew," she added, "was the Peeter Sirel of fifty years ago. Peeter has changed completely."

We lapsed into a thoughtful silence.

"Aleks put me in touch with Tofer, you know."

This time, the exchange of looks was very serious. Habermel's face seemed to have turned grey.

"What's the matter?"

"Over 1,200 Jews died in Vaivara concentration camp during the autumn of 1943," said Hilge quietly. "David's parents were among that 1,200. Tofer was one of the Estonian SS guards."

The wind moaned at the corner of the house. Habermel rose and walked over to the Stanley range. He inserted one of Hans's home-made tools into the groove in the top plate and lifted it. He gazed down, the reflected embers turning his face to molten stone. He dropped in four logs, unhurriedly in succession, and watched how the sparks rose. Hilge's voice, suddenly throaty with some deep emotion, cut into the silence.

"I promised Nadja, the day she died, that her story—Aleks's story—would be told. She *wanted* you to tell it."

"But—"

"The time was wrong, John! The circumstances were wrong. She knew you'd have to speak to Peeter. I promised to put you in touch with him. That is, if you still want to—"

"I do! But without restrictions or conditions! I meet anyone I need to meet, including Tofer."

Habermel firmly replaced the top plate. He resumed his seat as if he had suddenly gotten old, and Hilge grasped his hand.

"We spoke about this," Hilge now said solemnly. "David knows that you have to see Tofer. Peeter knows it too. He said that he would see you, in London, at anytime."

"Can I ask you something?" I asked Habermel.

"Yes?"

"Was it really Hans the Israeli government wished to honour?"

Hilge did not seem surprised, nor was she indignant. Habermel took his time.

"The person we all wanted to see honoured was Peeter Sirel, because he organized one of the most spectacular escapes of Jews during the War, aided by Hans. This could not be done because of Peeter's involvement in the arms trade. Besides, his membership in an SS division and his involvement with German intelligence made it all potentially embarrassing politically."

"It sounds to me as if there are at least two stories here!"

"It's all one story, John," said Hilge quietly. "Aleks was the only one who wrote an account of it. The problem always was that that story is much bigger than just the part that Aleks played."

"You seem to be saying that Peeter Sirel was in fact the main protagonist?"

"There are two," interjected Habermel solemnly, "the other being Zdanov."

"Will Peeter Sirel tell me everything?"

"Not only that!" said Hilge. "He will help you too."

I left shortly after that.

I met Sirel in London a week later. He told me he could give me only an hour that morning, as he was expecting someone, but that we could begin the interviews straight away.

"I should point out, however," said Sirel, "that my priority at this moment is not a war memoir but a satisfactory conclusion to negotiations with our Mr Zdanov."

The manner was sardonic, the voice all fruit and nut. It perfectly suggested the British military officer class in mufti. In repose, Sirel made no unnecessary movements. In motion, he reminded me of a leathery tiger. He had close-cropped, iron-grey hair and a clipped moustache. He wore a cravat, a lumpy cardigan, and half-moon reading glasses halfway down his nose. It was an act which the amused actor himself refused to take seriously. Whatever its purpose, Sirel's acting seemed to be directed from behind, giving an impression of contained power.

We were sitting either side of an ornate marble fireplace, on the top floor of a house in Hampstead. The room somehow suggested the library of a great country house. A large window overlooked the heath.

It was quiet as a church in there. The hum of the central heating complemented the ponderous labours of an ormolu clock. Distant voices and the yapping of a dog carried faintly on the wind.

"You don't know who Zdanov is, really, do you?"

"He was head of the—"

"Yes, he was. But do you know who he is now?"

"No, I don't."

Sirel gazed at me with that ironic expression. He sat upright, still and relaxed.

"At this moment, John, as we speak, a huge Soviet empire is breaking up. Emerging at the same time, to replace it, is a new capitalist empire run by shady export kings, launderers of Communist Party assets, and mafia running prostitution, drugs, and whatnot. And one squeaky-clean, idealistic politician thinks he can control all this—"

"You're talking about Gorbachev?"

"Yes! A thug in a business suit—Boris Yeltsin—who slept rough in railway carriages when he was young is waiting in the wings to take over. It's estimated that, in the last nine months alone, somewhere between $17 b. and $40 b. was illegally exported to Swiss banks. Simply stolen! That's what friend Zdanov is involved in. That doesn't stop him from coveting £4 m. sterling—as a personal nest egg—money which rightly belongs to Hilge."

He became quite still, gazing at me unblinkingly, as if weighing my quotient of being.

"That means," I said, "that whatever it is that you have, which he wants, must be pretty valuable."

Sirel smiled a slow, beatific smile.

"Let's just say that, remarkably for a man who has no principles, the recovery of this property from me has now become a matter of principle with him."

"You mean this property originally belonged to him?"

Sirel's face had suddenly acquired a curiously blank expression.

"You know this word 'serendipity'?" he enquired seriously.

I nodded.

"It means," he told me anyway, "the ability to make pleasant and unexpected discoveries entirely by chance." A hint of wicked humour momentarily lit his eyes. "It seems," he admitted modestly, "that I have this ability. The only problem is, our friend Zdanov seems to share the same gift."

"So what is it you have that he wants?"

"During the War, various national treasures went missing. One of these came into my possession. Zdanov seems to think it's his property."

"Is it?"

"That," said Sirel dryly, "is not even an issue anymore. Other factors have entered the equation."

He paused to fix me with a look. The eyes could suddenly go very cold and hard, with the ferocity of a hunting bird.

"Okay."

"The treasure in question was en route to the Soviet Union in 1945 when it went missing. Russia still holds Zdanov responsible for the loss."

"Why?"

"It was his responsibility. The Soviet Union considered the treasure to be legitimate war booty. On the other hand, should Zdanov manage to recover it, he would become something of a national hero—no, maybe not. They'd keep it all quiet. In any case, he would become a considerably richer man than he is already."

"How would he do that?"

"Various national institutions, particularly two museums—in St Petersburg and Moscow—would be very grateful to him."

"I didn't get the impression, from what you said, that Zdanov was an altruist."

"He's not. The treasure in question is, as they say, priceless. That doesn't mean that these institutions and Zdanov could not reach an agreement concerning a 'recovery fee.'"

"As I understand it, you have what he wants—he has what you want. What's holding up the negotiations?"

Sirel was reaching down, in his deliberate fashion, to extract a packet of cigarettes from a bureau drawer. As he looked up, he levelled on me a look of such bleakness that it seemed to go right through my solar plexus. There was something of Arthur Kass in it, but the intensity reminded me instantly of Hilge.

"Human nature," he murmured. "That's what holding them up."

In the ensuing silence, I watched every single movement of the process of lighting up. There was no physical resemblance, but something essential connected Sirel and Hilge. The smell of sulphur and fresh cigarette smoke enhanced the impression.

"No creature goes up to a lion and snatches fresh meat from between his claws. That's how Zdanov sees things. Getting the treasure back is not enough. He wants his pound and a half of flesh as well."

Someone far away, out on the heath, slammed a car door. It was a muffled sound from another world.

"There's another complication. I run a rather large fine arts and antiquities enterprise. I specialize in providing very rich people with rare pieces, which only they will ever view. I sold the treasure to one of those people and then had to buy it back."

"It seems to me that it would have been easier just to give the money to Hilge—"

I broke off, because he was nodding knowingly. He continued to gaze at me as an owl might at a mouse on a barn floor.

"And just forget about her inheritance?" he enquired rhetorically. I stared back, as the implications got through to me.

"So where is this treasure now?"

Suddenly, Sirel laughed, taking me by surprise and introducing a new mood. He tapped the side of his nose with a stiffened forefinger, in a distinctly Levantine gesture.

"My dear chap, there are governments, national institutions, museums the world over—not to mention a retired Russian general—who would give a lot to know the answer to that question!"

I shrugged. He sobered and surveyed me with darkly glowing eyes.

"It's in a safe place, believe me," he reassured me. He nodded to agree with himself.

We lapsed into silence again. I listened to the ormolu clock and the hum of the heating for a while.

"How does Zdanov intend to get his pound of flesh?"

Sirel turned the hunting-bird look on me. There seemed to be white areas at the corners of his mouth. I thought he'd never stop staring.

"I know some bankers here, John, in the city—American bankers. They know that, as soon as the new Russia sorts itself out, not only business but Russian banks are going to need huge injections of capital. They want to get in on the ground floor. But they want to know their money is safe. You know what they're doing?"

"What?"

"This *American* bank is hiring ex-KGB operatives to get advice on how best to recoup its loans in Russia, should things go wrong."

"What does it mean?"

"These KGB heavies were scared to talk about some of the people involved in the Russian banking world."

"What is your point?"

Sirel stared at me as if he hadn't heard. His face had acquired a blotched pallor.

"Last week, my people found an explosive device on the underside of my granddaughter's car—right outside in this street. It was fully primed but not connected to the engine. This was Zdanov showing he could get to us anytime he wanted. These are the kind of people we're dealing with."

I looked at him, aghast. We were silent for quite a while after that.

"What happens after Zdanov gets what he wants?"

"He wants to see me dead."

We were silent again for some time.

"Which national treasure are we talking about?"

Sirel came back from some distant place and sighed.

"You know the name Schliemann?"

"Schliemann? Should I? Schliemann, Schliemann . . ."

"He was an archeologist—"

"He discovered the gold of Troy—"

"Right, and we rediscovered it in the back of a truck on a forest road in Viljandi, Estonia, in 1945."

I stared at him. Hilge had warned me about his sense of humour. There was no humour in that expression.

"How could that be? Schliemann donated it to some museum in Germany, back in 18-something—"

"He donated it in fact, to the Volkerkundemuseum, Berlin, on 7 July 1881 at a royal reception attended by Crown Prince Wilhelm."

"So how did it get—"

"During the War, the treasure was removed and placed for safekeeping in a secret bunker below the Berlin Zoo. In 1945, some Russian soldiers discovered it, and . . ."

He trailed off and gazed at me thoughtfully. I had been nodding, partly to disguise some deep misgivings about the story.

"Okay," I said. "So Zdanov was the—what? Officer in charge of the—"

"NKVD, Special Operations."

"Did Zdanov have prior knowledge as to its location? And did you have prior knowledge as to its route back to Russia?"

Sirel was gazing at me thoughtfully, reading my doubt with no difficulty.

"We both knew about this treasure in Berlin. Stopping this truck on a road in Viljandi was a lucky accident—serendipity, perhaps. It's a long story, John."

His dry tone clearly precluded any further discussion of the subject, at least for the moment.

It was only in 1993, some two years after this conversation, that I learned the Russian authorities were admitting, for the first time, that they had the treasure. The following year, 1994, archaeologists were able to view the ceremonial axes, which formed part of the so-called Priam's Treasure, in Moscow's Pushkin Museum. The remainder of the treasure was kept at the Hermitage. The revelations plunged the famous museums into controversy. Germany immediately initiated proceedings to recover the stolen treasure. Russia maintained it was legitimate war booty, which they refused to return without compensation. The Greek culture minister was hoping to exhibit the artifacts in Athens in 1997. In 1998, Boris Yeltsin was still locked in a struggle with the Russian parliament over the treasure. The constitutional court declared it war booty.

"Habermel told me some of the reasons why Aleks did not want to put me in contact with you. Was there some fundamental difficulty between you?"

Sirel had been brought out of a deep reverie. Now he began to focus on me.

"Aleks," he began, "was a true leader of men. He had that knack of command, which so few men have. Germans gave him the Iron Cross in 1944, on the Russian Front, under his German name, Alois Kalls. Did you know that?"

I nodded.

"Where or how did you first meet?"

"It was in Finland, 1939, two days before Suomussalmi."

As darkness fell on the evening of 27 December 1939, journalist Peeter Sirel was on the waterfront of a small, blacked-out port on Finland's west coast. As the wailing of the sirens died away, the hundreds of mothers and their children listened intently to the drone of the Russian bombers, fading into the distant sky. Mindful of Stalin's extermination programmes, Finnish parents were using every available boat to get their children out to Sweden. The Russian troops had been issued with written warnings not to cross into Sweden once they had reached Finland's western border. The Soviet forces included a brass band for the victory parade in Helsinki.

One mother had sobbed hysterically throughout the raid, clutching her two little children fiercely into the front of her skirts.

All his life until that moment, Peeter Sirel had felt that he was only partially alive. He had a brain and a body, but it was as if his human feelings were dead. These feelings had been driven deep inside, repressed, and only a primordial, consuming anger was there. He was not Hilge's half-brother but her uncle's illegitimate son. He had been brought up with Hilge, Sasha, and their mother, and these three had never been anything but kind. It was the hypocritical dowager aunts and the hearty, sly uncles who had given him clearly to understand that he was—and would always be—a bastard.

He had removed himself from them all, taking only his anger. That night, that mother's sobbing did not just turn his anger in a different direction. It marked the beginning of his personal regeneration. It was to be a bloody and painful rebirth.

Very late that same night, when he arrived back in the Helsinki office, a car was waiting to take him to the south coast, to cover another story. The 3,000 or so Estonian volunteers, who had come by boat earlier in the month, did not in fact take part in the Winter War. They were to form the Estonian Legion. But now, several hundred more were crossing the thick ice, at the eastern end of the gulf. Russian planes strafed them by day. High-speed motorized sleighs harassed them by night, but still they came.

The blizzard was abating as Sirel arrived at the coast, near Borga. Far out on the ice, a battle was in progress. The noise from the Russian machine guns was tremendous, echoing back across the vast emptiness. Then the confused criss-crossing of searchlights steadied into three beams of light, moving steadily towards the coast, swerving occasionally, as if to avoid obstacles. It was the victorious Estonians in three captured Russian sleighs piled high with Russian guns and ammunition.

The man who got out of the first sleigh was clearly the leader. He introduced himself as Aleks Kallas. In the second sleigh was Johann Semmal. Tofer was in the third. There were six other men, four of them wounded.

When the captain of the Finnish border guard unit had taken charge of the wounded men, Kallas announced that he was taking the three sleighs back out on the ice.

"Why, for God's sake?" said the astonished captain.

"Because there are at least three more Russian sleighs out there."

"You're going with four men?"

"I'll need volunteers."

"I'll go!" said Peeter Sirel.

"Who the fuck are you?" asked Tofer, looking him up and down. Sirel told him. Tofer scoffed.

"Can you use one of these?" asked Tofer, shoving a German Schmeisser close to his face.

"I'll be able to when you show me!"

"Let's go!" exclaimed Kallas.

The border guard captain insisted on giving Kallas German machine guns to mount on the sleighs. They were much more accurate than the Russian ones. Three of the local Finns volunteered to go with them.

The fury of the Estonian attack astonished the Russians. Sirel shot two. One of them fell slowly sideways out of the sleigh, blood pumping from his neck. He took note of the fact that he felt nothing—a kind of curiosity, that's all.

The guns had fallen silent. Ten to twelve Russians were dead, as was one of the Finns. In the light of one of the searchlights, he saw a figure swiftly going from dead Russian to dead Russian, briefly lift the head by hair or collar and slit the throats with the professional indifference of a butcher. It was Tofer.

"What are you doing?"

"Making sure! You want a bullet in the back?"

"Gather round!" shouted Kallas. They formed a circle around him.

"Aarand," he said to Tofer, "collect the guns."

"Johann—the ammunition. And you," he said to Sirel, "collect the boots."

Sirel stared at him.

"Take them off the Russians' feet!" he commanded.

Then Sirel understood. The Finnish troops had been issued with poor-quality boots, often the wrong size. Thousands of men had been uselessly withdrawn from the front because of frostbite. The Russians had good-quality felt boots.

"According to this man—Matti Kovero—that I met in Ireland, Aleks Kallas fought at Suomussalmi—"

"We all did. It was only two days after that."

"How did you—"

"Aleks had thought of everything. He had brought enough pairs of skis for twenty men. There was an acute shortage of them. The Finnish troops were mostly on horses. The heavy, armoured Russian divisions had to stick to the roads. We formed a special unit, all on skis and in white camouflage. It was led by native Russian speakers like Tofer and Semmal to work behind enemy lines, always at night."

"Doing what?"

"Blowing up arms dumps, artillery, and transports, breaking down morale, taking prisoners."

He bowed his head as if concentrating on some memory, his face curiously blank.

"About eighty per cent of that entire special force—Estonians and Finns—did not survive the Winter War."

It was a solemn moment.

During the Winter War, Sirel learned the art of war from Kallas. From Tofer, he learned the art of silent killing and every trick of survival. His anger burned brightly, and he killed with indifference. The indifference extended to Sirel himself, because he realized that he didn't care if he lived or died.

The closest encounters with death gave glimpses of the real meaning of life. A new way of seeing things began, with a sudden realization that it was abnormal to feel nothing on witnessing the brutal extinction of a fellow human being. As he witnessed the terrible things that could happen to women and children, something like conscience, and with it at last, human feelings, began floating to the surface from a deep place.

He began to see war as a great obscenity. Not as something for which man was directly or wholly responsible, because he could no more control it than he could stop sap rising with the pull of the moon. But man was partially responsible, because there was something essentially evil or abnormal about his whole way of life, which attracted war, in much the same way as deforestation affecting climate.

"Did you return with Aleks on 5 January 1940?"

"Yes."

"What happened?"

"First of all, the newspaper I was working for had stopped printing my dispatches, because Estonia was officially supposed to be neutral. Secondly, Zdanov had emerged from the shadows. As de facto governor of Estonia, he presented President Päts with a list of new ministers he wanted in the government. Päts made minor changes, hoping to stall the Russians."

"What about Aleks, Hilge, Sasha, your family?"

The business community had been lulled into a false sense of security by their government. As a senior civil servant, Sasha Veinberg saw how already the police force, and in particular the political police, were being infiltrated. He, and now also his half-brother Peeter Sirel, strongly urged his parents to leave. But they held on stubbornly. President Päts was a personal friend. He had reassured them. They had too much to lose. They were still maintaining that position on 17 June when Russian soldiers marched into Estonia.

As soon as Colonel Hans Kersting of the Wehrmacht joined the German-USSR Joint Commission and met Hilge, Sasha was already planning to get her out. This did not happen until October 1940. By that time, everything had changed. The head of the Estonian political police, Tuulse, had ordered the destruction of the archives on anti-Soviet elements before he and his wife committed suicide. The man who actually carried out this destruction of files and replaced them with carefully crafted misinformation was senior civil servant Sasha Veinberg, a political appointee, favoured by the leader of the Estonian Left Socialist Party, Vares Barbarus. The latter was to become the new Prime Minister after the deportation of President Päts's legitimately elected government on 20 June 1940. From the moment of Tuulse's demise, Sasha Veinberg knew he was living on borrowed time.

"How did Aleks manage to survive in this situation?"

"Sasha warned Aleks that the best way to hide was 'in the system.' Aleks's business was nationalized, and he was fired from his own company. Sasha got him an administrative post in the housing executive—"

"But you went to Finland?"

"Yes. Immediately our government was deported on 20 June."

"Why?"

"Two reasons. Sasha had told me that it would be a matter of a month or two before Estonia was fully incorporated into the Soviet Union—that the situation was hopeless. And Hans Kersting told me about the secret draft in Finland to get volunteers for a Finnish SS battalion."

"What were your reasons for joining the SS?"

"Kersting told me that the SS were looking for 80-100 Estonians who would be specially trained and parachuted back into Estonia."

"If Hans Kersting knew in June 1940 about Hitler's plans to invade Russia the following summer, he had to have been in German intelligence."

"He was a high-ranking officer in the Abwehr, the intelligence service of the Wehrmacht. And he recruited me before I left for Finland."

"How does Aleks fit into this?"

"He was a major player in the overall plan."

"What plan?"

"Colonel Hans Kersting of the Wehrmacht, in fact of the Abwehr, was sent to Estonia, precisely to prepare the ground there for the invasion of Russia the following summer. His brief was to establish and maintain contact with strategically located pockets of resistance, with a view to facilitating the speedy passage through Estonia of German Army Group North under General von Leeb."

"So Aleks's group was nothing special, just one of many?"

"The German plan was that the SS-trained Estonians—myself included—would be parachuted in, on the day of invasion, to join designated resistance groups. I was assigned to Aleks's group, because it was about to play a key role."

"Why didn't Aleks want me to meet you?"

"Do you know who Alfons Rebane was?"

"Of course: the Estonian SS commander!"

"There's the key to your mystery. Aleks had good reason to protect his version of events."

ᏎᏬᎾ

Chapter 4

❦

"**D**ID ALEKS HAVE something to hide?"

"When war ends, John, the victors get to write the official histories. The losers are bad news, their allies tarred with the same brush. Aleks felt that what he believed in and had fought for did not deserve that."

In July 2002, a group of ex-servicemen announced their intention to unveil a monument—featuring a soldier in Estonian Waffen SS uniform—which was meant to pay tribute to all those who had died fighting for their country against the tyranny of Stalin. Prime Minister Siim Kallas had condemned the move, saying it would tarnish the country's image. Estonia was seeking EU and NATO membership that year. Memories were still fresh concerning the indignant reaction of the American Jewish Congress to the reburial in 1998, with honours, of Alfons Rebane, in the national cemetery.

"What was Rebane's significance?"

"He was a rabid Nazi, who sent thousands of Russians and Jews to their deaths in Belzec and Vaivara concentration camps."

"What else?"

"Officially, Rebane is supposed to have been the leader of Estonian national resistance against the Soviets."

"Was he?"

"Rebane was a military man, a self-advertiser, later a puppet of British intelligence. He was the public face for what men like Aleks did."

"What exactly did Aleks do?"

"Because of his reputation and because of his strategic position in the south of the country, his group was singled out for a special three-stage mission—first, to set up targets from the ground for the Luftwaffe. They were then to act as a special unit, advancing northward, to prevent the sabotage of installations and infrastructure and, third, to enter and secure Tallinn ahead of Army Group North."

"German Army records make no mention of this."

"It happened," grated Sirel. "I was there! You've heard of rewriting history?"

"Did you meet Rebane?"

"Oh yes!" he exclaimed, smiling mysteriously. "Many times, during and after the War."

"In what connection?"

"It's very simple. Rebane was enthusiastic about the handful of Estonians specially trained by the SS. He asked Hans to introduce me to him."

"Did Rebane know about the connection with German Intelligence?"

"Yes. He knew we were both Abwehr. Rebane in his turn wanted me to meet a very special lady, an impoverished Baltic baroness whose family name had been, I believe, Schambok. She had chosen—at least temporarily—to drop the *particule nobiliaire* and become simply Schambok, Irma Schambok.

"What was her significance?"

"Irma was spoiled, overeducated, and at a loose end. Rebane saw her as the perfect person to identify, or 'sniff out,' rich and important Jewish families, with a view to their extermination."

"Did she not recognize you as a member of an important Jewish family?"

"I came back with a new identity. When the Einsatzgruppen started the hunt for Jews, they eventually found some 1,200 that Sasha had no time to provide for."

"What happened to the 1,200?"

"Taken to Belzec concentration camp. Not one survived."

"And what happened to the 3,000 he had provided for?"

"They were put on full alert, just prior to the German invasion."

"I don't understand."

"The list of 3,000 names had been confided to the care of Hans Kersting. Hans and I were in Finland immediately prior to the invasion. We were in contact with Aleks. Aleks had agreed to coordinate and facilitate the travel to his own base in the Viljandi swamps, in the south, of about 2,000 people, mostly women and children. But first, they were to volunteer to help the Russians defend Tallinn."

I looked at Sirel in astonishment. His expression was grave, almost sad. Had Hilge and Habermel not given me some indication of the story, I would have found it incredible.

"These people were Jews?"

"Yes."

"How were they got out?"

"Those from Viljandi were taken in open trucks, supposedly as volunteers, towards Tallinn, to work on building the city's outer defences. The truck drivers wore militia uniform. Their papers and instructions had all been put together by Sasha and Hans. All this happened over a four-day period, immediately after the German invasion, when everything was in a state of confusion and panic."

"But how did they get out of Estonia?"

"There's a small village called Vasala, on the west coast, not far from the town of Haapsalu, where one of our Winter War veterans had a fishing boat. There's a bridge across to the island of Saaremaa, but it was too well guarded. The Vasala fisherman took them over by boat at night—from there, through Finland, and on to Sweden."

"If 2,000 were got out, that leaves another 1,000. What happened to them?"

"These were the younger men. Some 600 of them were incorporated into Aleks's resistance group. The other 400 or so were put to work with local farmers we could trust."

"That's incredible! What happened to all those people?"

"Aleks escaped to Sweden himself through Vasala in 1944. About 500 of the Jewish partisans who survived went with him. Some stayed in Sweden, some went to Israel, the majority to the United States."

"And the other 400 or so worked on the farms?"

"Many joined the 'Forest Brothers,' who went on fighting the Soviets in Estonia up to 1956. We got about 200 of them out, with the help of British Intelligence."

"Sorry?"

"After 1945, British Intelligence—actually SIS—ran their famous Operation Jungle in Estonia. Their main agent in this was former Nazi Alfons Rebane. Rebane unwittingly facilitated the removal from Estonia of the national treasure we discussed, a quantity of gold bullion, and some 200 Jews."

Sirel leaned back with a deep sigh, the old ironic expression in place.

"Where does this lady you mentioned, Irma—"

"Schambok. Irma Schambok."

Sirel stared at me with a strange intensity.

"It's important to understand," he continued in a different voice, "the kind of person Irma was, and is."

"You mean she's still alive?"

"Very much so. She's living in Austria, married to Tofer. She's now Irma Tofer."

I stared at him. There was an ironic glint in his eye.

"Irma had lived her entire life in busy idleness, kicking her heels in the provinces. She longed for a real function, the big 'role.' And she had a deep-seated wish to enjoy again the wealth that generations of her family had enjoyed."

He paused and looked at me expectantly.

"So?"

"Hans Kersting understood all this. He understood also the danger she posed to us all while she stayed in Rebane's shadow."

"What did he do?"

"He took diversionary action."

"What does that mean?"

"It means that, with Rebane's backing, Hans managed to recruit her into the Abwehr, and got her sent to Berlin for training."

Sirel clearly was enjoying the memory of that manoeuvre.

"So what happened?"

"Irma was a huge success with the whole Nazi hierarchy. She got to play her role of Baltic baroness up to the hilt. She got to meet them all, Hitler, Göring—the whole outfit."

"Was that good or bad?"

"It exceeded even Hans's expectations and threw his calculations out somewhat."

"What had he calculated?"

Sirel examined me as if looking for something.

"Hans was hoping to plant her in the German Embassy in Helsinki, as our 'official' contact with Finnish Intelligence."

"Does the word 'official' have some special connotation here?"

"It does. We needed an 'official' contact, to cover for the 'unofficial' contact, which was in fact the business end of things."

"And who was that?"

"It was me, in fact. I was the direct contact with Marshal Mannerheim."

It was a flat statement, delivered with indifference or modesty. It was difficult to tell which.

"What's the point of this story?"

"The point is that it was Irma who discovered, during a weekend at Göring's hunting lodge, the proposal to build a bunker under the Berlin Zoo. And the plans to lodge Schliemann's Trojan treasure there—"

We were interrupted by the sound of a door slamming down below. It sounded like the hall door. This was followed by the excited yapping of a small dog.

"That'll be Angela," Sirel said.

"Sorry?"

"My granddaughter—back with the dog."

A door opened and then slammed. More excited yapping and then nothing. In the quiet, we heard the deep, muted tones of masculine voices, exchanging briefly and then a bright, cheerful, female voice and athletic running up the stairs. The door behind me burst open.

"Grandpops, I'm back! Oh, hello!" she said on seeing me. To Sirel, she said, "Am I interrupting something?"

She was tallish, slim, and blonde, very attractive and charming. The voice modulation and inflection were a good advertisement for expensive English boarding schools.

"Not in the least, my dear! This young man and I were just finishing—for the moment anyway."

There was a discreet knock on the door, and a big man came in quietly.

"They're here!" he announced cryptically.

Two more men came in behind him. The big man went to the window and looked down. The others joined him. Soon everyone was staring down, immobile.

Sirel turned to glance at me and remarked ironically, "John here is not quite sure if Zdanov even exists!"

Suddenly, I became the focus of attention. I walked over and looked down. Four cars were drawn up in tight formation, straddling the pavement. Their slightly tilted position suggested a great shiny-black articulated insect. The end section showed the discreet disc of the Corps Diplomatique.

Two men in crumpled suits had just got out. One had dark glasses and was mouthing something into a walkie-talkie. Both kept a wary eye up and down the street. The scene reminded me of Mafia films I'd seen.

A door in one of the middle cars opened, and a stocky figure got out. He wore a nondescript, dark-blue suit. I caught a glimpse of a red, unhealthy face and bushy eyebrows. He reminded me vaguely of Leonid Brezhnev. He walked around the car with a curious, stiff, jerky walk and disappeared into the building we occupied.

"Is that Zdanov?" I asked.

I got a few looks, but nobody answered. It was clear that it was. No one moved. Sirel rattled out something cryptically in Estonian, and they all nodded seriously, including Angela. Everyone was calm as if they knew exactly what to do.

"Vladi will take you to the airport," Sirel said to me. They were all looking at me again.

"Thank you."

Sirel turned to the big man, Vladi. The ironic smile was in place, the eyes cold.

"John has informed me that he is planning a visit to Austria next week, to meet your old friend Tofer."

Suddenly, I was fixed in Vladi's cold, assessing stare. The look was surprisingly like Sirel's.

"Let's go," said Vladi dryly.

There was a similar convoy of cars drawn up in a parallel street, with similar drivers and minders. Angela was placed in one of the middle cars. I found myself in the back seat of the front vehicle, beside Vladi. We moved off in silence, everyone on high alert.

The streets glided by with cinematic unreality. Vladi turned to me, his hand extended with grave courtesy.

"Vladi Lepp," he announced.

Chapter 5

⌀⟆⟆⟆⟆⟆⟆

"WHAT WAS GOING on back there with Zdanov?" I asked. Life outside the car sped by with a curious irrelevance. People and buildings, presented like flash cards, were whisked away.

"Negotiations," said Vladi dryly and gazed pointedly out to his left.

There was a peculiarly tense silence in the car. I met the driver's look in the mirror. There was a glint in the hard, bright button eyes as if he were gauging the effect on me. I realized that Vladi was manipulating the atmosphere in the car. He did it as easily as someone turning up a thermostat a few degrees. To what purpose, I had no way of knowing. It suddenly struck me that the three men in the car all had that offhand arrogance of professional minders, or top security men. A coded message emanated from this attitude: "Have you got the bottle—have you got what it takes to get involved in this game?" The implication was that it was the only game in town, and they were playing it all their own way.

"I tell you what, Vladi," I said, "I love heroics. There's nothing I like better than John Wayne aboard a horse, with the reins in his teeth, both guns spitting justice, and galloping forward to kick the shite out of the villains."

I waited for Vladi and the driver to exchange one of their quick-touch looks in the mirror. They weren't quite sure this time which game was being played. The big man in the front passenger seat showed no reaction. He was in another world.

"Especially," I continued, "when I have a bag of potato crisps in one hand and a bottle of Guinness in the other."

The eyes in the mirror crinkled slowly, and the driver laughed softly. Vladi was starting a big, slow grin.

"Toivo here," said Vladi, "is a great admirer of the Irish sense of humour. By the way, this is Toivo."

Toivo took his right hand off the wheel and reached back over his left shoulder to shake hands.

"Excuse me if I don't turn around," he said, eyes glimmering. He had a surprisingly strong voice for a little man. Immediately, something stirred in my subconscious, and questions began to surface.

"Aleks mentioned a sixteen-year-old sniper called Toivo—"

"Who shot Zdanov," Vladi cut in, nodding deeply, a strange little smile on his face.

"Yes! That's him!"

Toivo was nodding too, glancing at us solemnly in the mirror.

"If I'd got the bastard in the head," he said regretfully to Vladi in the mirror, "your family would still be alive."

Vladi turned aside, suddenly saddened, to gaze out at a passing world. I was struck by the respect, even affection, between the two men. The front-seat passenger, sensing something, asked a question in Russian. He got a laconic response which seemed to satisfy him. I turned to Vladi.

"I take it, from what Sirel said, that Tofer is no friend of yours?"

There was a sharp exchange of looks in the mirror.

"Tofer wiped out Vladi's family," Toivo murmured and then told me this story.

When Aleks Kallas had escaped to Sweden in September 1944 with the main resistance group, Vladi Lepp and his young cousin Toivo had chosen to fight on with the partisans in the Viljandi region of Sakkala province. These were the men who became known as the "Forest Brothers." Toivo was astonished, one day in February 1945, to see their leader, Johann Semmal, walk into their forest camp accompanied by two men he thought he'd never see again—Peeter Sirel and Aarand Tofer.

Toivo unexpectedly halted the narrative flow and scrutinized me in the mirror. I was aware of Vladi watching too. Images from Aleks's manuscript fast-forwarded through my brain, trying to register something.

"But Sirel was in Sweden, being tried on suspicion of murdering Corporal Eduard Poom!" I exclaimed.

Vladi and Toivo were both busily nodding, apparently in satisfaction.

"He was acquitted," murmured Vladi dryly.

"Then he turns up in Estonia again," said Toivo to the mirror, "with his mate Tofer."

There was an ironic twinkle in his eye.

"What happened?" I asked. Vladi took up the narrative.

As the Russians advanced into Estonia in early September 1944, Aleks Kallas's Twentieth Estonian SS Division fought a bloody rearguard action, which reduced his force to some 900 men. Officers of the Third SS Korps were everywhere, checking papers and arresting or even shooting suspected deserters. Some 500 of Kallas's men were Jews, survivors of the original 600 incorporated into the partisans. In addition to the new sets of papers furnished by Sasha Veinberg, each of these men carried an SS Sonderbefehl (special order) form, properly sealed, and signed by an SS Gruppenführer Vollherr, authorizing them to travel to the village of Vasala on the west coast, where they were to take up defensive duties.

The Sonderbefehl had been procured by Sirel. The signatures and seals were genuine, authorizing the holders to use available transport and to draw marching rations. The actual orders and the destination were written in by Kallas. This arrangement had been worked out long in advance, in order to be able to deal with any eventuality. Hans Kersting had warned Sirel in early July that Aleks Kallas's battalion was to receive orders to sail for Germany. Kallas had been advised to get out to Sweden during the retreat. He was to rendezvous with Sirel and Kersting in Tallinn en route, having procured a number of trucks. This he did with a heavy heart, not knowing or caring what the purpose was, preoccupied only with the news that Nadja—along with thousands of others—had been shipped to Germany as forced labour. More than a year was to pass before they would meet again.

Sirel meanwhile, from his office on Viru Street, was directing what was intended to be his last operation in Estonia. A quantity of gold bullion, worth millions of marks, was en route by rail to Tallinn, destined for Germany. Hans Kersting, who was responsible for its safe transfer there, had ordered that it be met at a station outside the city, and escorted by special SS detail to the Port of Tallinn. To that end he had ordered—through the good offices of the SS commander Alfons Rebane—that a special handpicked Estonian SS unit be released from their duties at Vaivara concentration camp. He had specially requested that SS Hauptscharführer Aarand Tofer be put in charge. Sirel and Kersting had agreed that this gold—stolen by Nazis in any case—should be diverted to Sweden via Vasala to fund the escapees in their new lives. Tofer and Poom were to link up with Aleks and escort the bullion to the coast.

Several things happened in quick succession to frustrate these plans.

That morning, as Sirel prepared to rendezvous with Tofer at the train, a crack regiment of Russian paratroops was dropped into Pelgullin, near the Port of Tallinn. From Staff HQ, Hans Kersting received orders to fall back with the main body of troops.

The gold was abandoned. Sirel, Tofer, and Kallas got to Sweden. Hans Kersting became part of the flotsam of war in a defeated Germany, but not for long. As soon as the Americans set up the first postwar intelligence service at the Oberursel army camp near Frankfurt in 1946, intelligence chief Reinhard Gehlen remembered the brilliant young Hans Kersting who knew Estonia so well. Within weeks of his recruitment, Kersting was on his way to Sweden, to establish a "werewolf" radio contact in Estonia with the help of Peeter Sirel. He was not to know that Sirel had been put on trial for murder, had been acquitted, and had returned to Estonia. Unexpectedly, former resistance leader Aleks Kallas had offered to go back into Estonia, on condition that the Americans find Nadja. She was found in a matter of weeks, in the British sector, whilst Kallas was in Viljandi.

In the meantime, in the space of one week, Hans Kersting found, proposed to, and married Hilge Veinberg in Stockholm. She had been in a displaced persons camp. They were astonished, and delighted, to learn of a last-minute arrival in the back of the church—Hilge's half-brother, Peeter Sirel, back from Estonia.

The young couple returned to Germany, and Sirel returned to Viljandi. He seemed able to come and go as he pleased, a man with some undeclared mission. British Intelligence—SIS—in pursuing the aims of Operation Jungle, dispatched former Nazi Alfons Rebane to meet him in Sweden in March 1946. The deal struck between them involved a commitment on the part of SIS to extricate some 200 Jews from the Viljandi area. British Intelligence was also persuaded to become involved in what came to be known in intelligence circles as Operation Agamemnon. This involved bringing Sirel himself out of Estonia, along with a consignment of very valuable artifacts—in fact, from ancient Troy. Neither British Intelligence nor Alfons Rebane ever learned of Sirel's separate arrangement with CIA operative William Smith O'Brien. But that was another story.

Vladi paused to look at me. I had two questions I needed answers to.

"Hilge and Kersting?"

"Returned to Germany," said Vladi flatly.

"They didn't live happily ever after," Toivo murmured to the mirror.

When the Kerstings moved from the "refugee camp" atmosphere of Oberursel to more comfortable quarters at Pullach in Bavaria, Hilge seemed much happier. Hans was climbing steadily up through the ranks of the "Bureau." What he never understood was her deep sense of isolation, her loneliness, her fundamental sense of loss. When she learned in 1949 that Aleks and Nadja were reunited and were living in Ireland, she became obsessed with the idea of moving there.

"So?"

Vladi shrugged.

"So he gave up his job. They moved."

I could see that I wasn't asking the questions they wanted me to ask.

"I still don't understand Tofer's part in all this. What was he doing back in Estonia with Sirel?"

"You remember that trainload of gold bullion? It wasn't exactly abandoned."

"Sirel and Tofer," said Toivo, "came to a gentlemen's agreement concerning the disposal of that particular asset."

The irony was a good imitation of Sirel's style. Toivo was clearly pleased with the choice of words.

"How did they come to that agreement?"

"With considerable difficulty," said Vladi with dark humour.

"Not to mention considerable protest and protestations of innocence on Tofer's part," said Toivo. I recognized Sirel's narrative style again in the remark.

"He maintained that he was innocent of what? You mean pressure was brought to bear on him?"

"He was given the third degree," said Vladi. He stared at me bleakly.

It took a few seconds for the implications to sink in.

"You mean he was tortured? By Sirel?"

I looked from one to the other in horror. Both faces had acquired identical blank expressions. Toivo kept glancing in the mirror as if running checks on me.

"Would it surprise you," said Vladi, "if I told you that Aleks was often obliged to employ such methods during the War?"

His manner was distant and formal, suggestive of a suave, prosecuting counsel. I stared at him, not knowing what to say.

They let the silence run for a while, and then Toivo said, softly and persuasively, "You ever turn over some old rubbish, John, and accidentally put your hand on a big, brown rat?"

Immediately, I felt the heat in my forehead and the sweat on my neck. I was seven years old, alone, on the canal banks. Two huge brown rats slithered away slowly from under the sack. One paused and looked back at me calmly. He was totally unafraid, his look insolent and calculating.

Toivo was watching me closely in the mirror. His strange, beaky lips parted slowly in what looked like a smile, and his front teeth looked like a rodent's.

"Their soft fur slithering along your arm, sinking their teeth into the bones of your hand."

I stared back calmly, aware of the shirt tail sticking wetly to the base of my spine.

"They're suddenly springing off the ground," he said softly, "leaping straight for your throat. What do you do?"

The short, glassy stares seemed to fix me. Now he was nodding as if he could see what I was seeing. One thing had now been settled—we both knew what I'd do if I saw those rats coming for my throat.

"What actually happened?" I asked. My voice was dry and cracked.

Vladi took his time. The atmosphere in the car seemed to relax somewhat.

The internment camp near Västervik, on the Swedish mainland, stood on elevated ground near the sea. There was a sheer drop of some 150 feet to the rocky shore. When the Swedish military patrol found the bleeding, broken body of Scharführer Eduard Poom there the morning after the arrival of the Estonians, it was assumed that he had overindulged at the welcoming party the night before and fallen to his death. The police, however, quickly established that he had been tortured and thrown over. Several of the men questioned attested to Sirel's ruthless behaviour towards rapists, looters, and arsonists during the retreat in Estonia. They cited instances in which he had shot men out of hand for disobeying orders. Poom had been questioned by Sirel on suspicion of rape. The police could not have known that Tofer had been busy, inciting the malcontents for his own purposes. Sirel was arrested on suspicion of murder, tried, and acquitted for lack of sufficient evidence.

Vladi brought the narrative to an abrupt halt as before, and looked at me.

"So who killed Poom?"

"Tofer did."

"Why?"

"The evening after the trial," said Toivo into the mirror, "Sirel, Vladi, and I interviewed Tofer, in the privacy of some nearby woods, with the purpose of establishing the facts of the case."

"I have to say," said Vladi, with heavy irony, "that he made a full and honest confession."

I looked from one to the other. Toivo was nodding grimly into the mirror.

"You tortured him?"

Vladi's eyes had gone very cold.

"'Third degree' is the correct technical term," he rasped. "And don't give me any prissy crap about human rights! We're talking about vermin here!"

Toivo was busily nodding at me in the mirror.

"Our little furry friends," he said dreamily. He gave me a look in the mirror that brought a shiver across my shoulders.

"It was a case," continued Vladi, "of thieves falling out."

"Over the gold?"

"What else!"

The operation at the railway station had gone like clockwork. The Wehrmacht had already loaded the first two trucks from the train when Sirel's instructions to abort the mission came in on the field transmitter. Hauptscharführer Tofer quickly made up his mind. The Wehrmacht troops were told to try to get everything into two trucks. Tofer went with the first truck, Poom with the one behind. A couple of kilometres down the forest road, Tofer knew they'd never make the rendezvous in Tallinn. The trucks were overloaded and unstable. He drove into a clearing among the trees, where there was an old sawmill. In exchange for a thick wad of Russian roubles, the old man who owned it agreed to provide secure storage for a few days. Under a bench on which the circular saw was mounted was a trapdoor leading to a miniature cellar where the old man hid alcohol and food from the requisitions of the militia. The old man and his son watched in astonishment as the four SS troopers went back and forth, filling his cellar with gold bars from the truck. As soon as the bench was back in place, Tofer and Poom mowed down the four SS men, the old man, and his son with their Schmeissers. The son's wife and three children, in the house nearby, met with the same fate.

I looked from one to the other. They had both become deeply thoughtful.

"There's something personal between you and Tofer, isn't there?"

Vladi stared at me, and Toivo watched.

"Yes, there is," Vladi said.

It was Toivo, however, that took up the story.

Something had occurred in Germany, which marked Irma Schambok for life. At Cairnhall, Hermann Göring's hunting lodge in the forest of Shorfheide in East Prussia, she first learned of the plan to build a secret bunker under the Berlin Zoo and to lodge Schliemann's famous Trojan treasure there. During her last weekend at Cairnhall, she was not only shown but was asked to wear some of the jewellery from the treasure for the benefit of the special guests. From that moment, she became obsessed with the idea of possessing the treasure at whatever cost.

As Allied bombs rained down and the city disintegrated around her, Irma insisted on holding on in Berlin. Kersting urged her to get out and take up her position in the German Embassy in Helsinki. She could not leave until she was sure that Göring had left the city. The treasure was safe for the moment beneath the rubble. She left on 4 February 1945, just five days before Zhukov's First Belorussian Front crossed the Oder and started coming in through the suburbs.

From Helsinki, she immediately went to Sweden to put a proposition to Sirel concerning the treasure. Kersting had been invaluable in getting her out of Germany, but she had not confided in him concerning the hoard beneath the zoo. In her opinion, Kersting lacked the requisite ruthless ingenuity of Sirel. He had agreed, however, to remain in radio contact and to keep her posted on developments in Germany.

Sirel, she found, had other things on his mind. He had just been acquitted of the charge of murder and was preparing to go back into Estonia. When he checked with Kersting, he learned that the Tiergarten borough, where the zoological gardens were, had already been overrun by the Russians. In the circumstances, Sirel considered Irma's proposition not only nonviable but even bizarre.

At this point, Irma had turned to Tofer. Between them, they hatched an outrageous plan to get possession of the treasure in Berlin. In a way, the plan was simplicity itself. With feminine logic, backed by the force of her obsession with the jewellery she had worn at Cairnhall, she had concluded that, since Tofer was a native Russian speaker from the city of Narva, up near the Russian border, he must know someone in the Russian armies heading for Berlin. At first, Tofer was amused at her simplicity and dismissed her idea out of hand. Then he realized that he did know someone, someone very important, from his home town of Narva—Andrei Zdanov, formerly head of the NKVD in Estonia, originally of the trade delegation at the Soviet Embassy, and subsequently, de facto ruler of Estonia, architect of the Russian takeover and the deportation of President Päts's government.

"I didn't know there was a connection between Tofer and Zdanov."

"Oh yes, there is!" said Toivo cheerfully into the mirror. Vladi was nodding.

"You can ask him all about it when you see him next week," he said grimly.

"What was this personal thing with Tofer?"

Vladi suddenly looked away, ignoring me. It was Toivo who answered, gravely, keeping an eye on Vladi.

"The old man and his son who were killed by Tofer at the sawmill were Vladi's father and brother. His sister-in-law was raped before she died. The three little children . . ."

He trailed off. He shot several looks in Vladi's direction then concentrated on his driving.

To me, it was almost inconceivable that a woman with Irma Schamboks's background could become involved with a man like Tofer. According to Toivo, however, when it came to basic instincts, Tofer proved to be the fatal attraction for the impoverished baroness, scion of an effete lineage.

"How does Zdanov fit into all this?"

"Sirel and Tofer are back in Viljandi with the partisans in February 1945, right?" said Toivo.

"Right."

"Zdanov is back in Tallinn, so Tofer goes to meet him."

"It was as simple as that?"

"Yes, it was!" He nodded.

"Did Sirel know the purpose of the trip?"

"He did when Tofer returned. With a story specially cooked up by Zdanov and his mate Tofer."

"What happened?"

"Tofer is inducted into the NKVD as a special agent and accompanies Zdanov to Berlin."

He paused. I felt that they were both watching me.

"That's bizarre," I said.

The nodded sympathetically, and Vladi said, rather gravely, "It's bizarre. But that's what happened."

I took a few moments to digest it.

"Did Sirel become involved in this?"

Vladi took his time before answering, "If you want to begin to understand Zdanov's mentality, think of an onion—layer after layer of skin. The centre of that onion is the ultimate goal."

"You need a mind like Sirel's to work it all out," remarked Toivo.

"Tell me what happened."

Vladi was winding down the window. He extracted a packet of cigarettes from a pocket and noisily undid the cellophane wrapper. Toivo was staring hard at him in the mirror, looking cross. He said something in Estonian and got an equally sharp reply from Vladi, who was holding the plumed flame of a lighter up to the cigarette in his mouth.

The big man in the front passenger seat stirred and asked something laconically in Russian. Toivo's reply was terse. The big man nodded ponderously but made no comment.

With the first intake of smoke, Vladi began a horrible coughing which went on and on. The cigarette burned right down with a long appendage of ash sticking up between the index and middle finger of his right hand, which remained curiously immobile on his knee.

At last, the horrible coughing stopped. Vladi was leaning towards the open window, gasping and white as a sheet. He was clearly a very sick man. He was neat as a pin, with his black overcoat, matching silk scarf, and leather gloves. He had a full head of iron-grey hair, slicked back with an old-fashioned pomaded look. He must have been in his sixties. All three men, in fact, gave the curious impression of being relics of another more formal era.

Cutting through the deeply thoughtful atmosphere, I said, addressing Toivo, "So Zdanov and Tofer get to Berlin. What happens then?"

Toivo visibly made an effort to focus on the matter in hand.

"They dig out the treasure. Zdanov had thought of everything. He went though all the proper channels, reporting the 'discovery' of the Schliemann treasure—thanks, of course, to his intelligence network—to the proper authority in Moscow and then arranged to have it shipped back east as legitimate 'war booty.'"

He checked in the mirror for my reaction, and his ironic expression was back in place.

"But how could he have profited from that?"

Instead of answering, Toivo gave me a long, ironic look. It was Vladi who replied. He was still white. He remained motionless, and his lips moved with a curious, stiff action.

"Zdanov was covering himself. All the paperwork was in order. He was provided with three trucks and a military escort."

"Why three trucks?"

Toivo nodded deeply in the mirror.

"What the pen-pushers back in Moscow fail to understand," he said, "is that this famous treasure we're talking about takes up only part of one truck."

"What was in the other two?"

"Paintings, valuable silver, jewellery—there was a lot more in that bunker than just the Schliemann treasure—"

"Did Zdanov know about this beforehand?"

"Of course he knew! You think Zdanov could be persuaded to go to all that trouble just to collect a bunch of antique junk which only a museum would want?"

"What about his agreement with Tofer and Irma?"

"Aha!" exclaimed Toivo, as if in triumph. "That's where Zdanov's whole scheme went haywire."

"Which scheme was that?"

It was Vladi who answered. He was looking a bit better.

"The brass in Moscow," he said, "are persuaded that the safest route for the treasure is overland through Estonia. They are not informed that the convoy is scheduled to be attacked by partisans en route. And that, in spite of putting up a tremendous fight, the military escort will get back to Leningrad with only one truck, which contains the famous treasure—"

"And a bunch of old paintings," added Toivo, "all dark varnish and gold."

"Is that what happened?"

"That's exactly what happened," said Toivo.

"What about the other two trucks?"

"They disappear without trace," said Vladi flatly.

Toivo added a qualifier.

"That is, so far as the authorities back home in Russia are concerned."

"Are you telling me that Sirel went along with this bizarre scheme?"

Toivo glanced at me quickly. His tone suddenly became more sober.

"Zdanov knew by then who Sirel was. He was sure he had convinced him—through Tofer—to stage this ambush, in return for a fifty-fifty share of the proceeds.

"Zdanov is vermin. With a mind like a corkscrew stuck in his head. The real plan is to wipe out all the partisans, which is why the escort is made up of top-notch Russian paratroopers. In the confusion, Tofer and the NKVD heavies are to disappear with the two trucks—"

"But," interpolated Vladi, "Sirel has anticipated all this. His plan is remarkably similar to Zdanov's—wipe out all these schmucks and take the two trucks himself."

"So?"

"The front truck, where the treasure is, is jam-packed with paratroopers. It shoots ahead, destination Leningrad."

"Meanwhile," said Toivo, "back in the woods, there's a big shoot-out. Three of Sirel's best go down, four of the paras. In the end, the paras take off with one of the trucks; Sirel gets the other. Who's at the wheel but our old friend Tofer. Sirel grants him a private interview, at the end of which Tofer decides that his best interests lie with Sirel after all."

"What about Zdanov?"

"Zdanov wasn't there. Tofer was in charge. Zdanov is already in Leningrad, talking to museum curators, waiting for the kudos to descend like gentle rain."

"Instead," said Vladi, "what settles on him begins to smell like a bad egg. First, he learns from the NKVD that Sirel had anticipated his every move. He loses face with his cronies. He goes crazy, because no one but no one gets the better of Zdanov."

"Worst of all," said Toivo, "was what happened when the curator of the museum in Leningrad started going through the Schliemann treasure."

"Why?"

"Part of the treasure was missing."

"What was the significance of that?"

"The curator claimed that the treasure could never be exhibited incomplete, and Zdanov was held responsible."

"But how did it happen?"

"Tofer—the joker in the pack—screwed everything up by keeping a promise he had made to Irma."

"What promise?"

"He promised her that—no matter what happened—he would get her the diadem from the treasure that she had worn at Cairnhall."

"But how?"

"Just as the shoot-out begins, Tofer orders the front truck to wait while he offloads the diadem in question. Trouble is there are two of these diadems. Tofer is confused, so he grabs both. Just for good measure, he grabs anything else that looks like a diadem or a necklace. Meanwhile, bullets are flying. The first truck barely gets away in time, the second truck was just lucky, and Tofer is hardly behind the wheel of his truck when Sirel closes in."

We sped along in silence. Through the rear window, I saw the other two cars following in close formation.

"You never mentioned the gold," I said, "that Sirel and Tofer had come back to Estonia for."

Toivo had been in deep thought. Now he looked in the mirror as if remembering that I was there.

"The gold was not forgotten," he said quietly. "It was still there, under the sawmill floor."

"And what about the truckload of valuables that Sirel had captured?"

"Aleks Kallas drove it down to his home place at Kalda, in the heart of the Viljandi swamplands," said Vladi.

I looked from one to the other.

"How were all these things connected?"

Toivo heaved a deep sigh but gave me a tolerant look.

"This is where things get a little complicated," he said.

"Pride," murmured Vladi, "ferocious pride, is like an axle around which everything else in Zdanov's character turns—"

"He's a big, brown, arrogant, greedy rat," said Toivo, "totally indifferent to the lives of other people."

"After being outsmarted in the forest, the destruction of Sirel became the central obsession of his life."

"What form did the obsession take?"

"The NKVD hit the whole Viljandi area like a rain of shrapnel. Those with any connection to the partisans just disappeared. Men brought in for questioning were found lying in the street, minus hands or fingers, or with broken legs. It went on for a whole year."

"Paratroopers rained down on the swamps. Trying to get at the enclave in Kalda."

"What happened?"

"The 'Forest Brothers'—under Sirel, Kallas, and Johann— ambushed them, blew them up, gunned them down, knifed them at night. Or they just drowned them in the mud holes. Then it all stopped."

"Why?"

"That was hard to tell. But Zdanov wasn't all powerful. There were some in the Kremlin who would probably have refused to continue funding Zdanov's private vendetta in Viljandi."

"What happened then?"

"Zdanov tried negotiating with Sirel."

"Tell me something."

"Yes?"

"How did the partisans—the 'Forest Brothers'—get the firepower to conduct a war like this? I mean, who funded them?"

"British intelligence did. SIS. But that's another story."

"Who made the first move in the negotiations?"

"Zdanov did, because he was certain he could still outsmart Sirel."

"Did he?"

"The move put Sirel in a quandary. As a precaution, Zdanov demanded that all the missing items from the treasure be returned to him. He was sure that he and Sirel could then work out some deal concerning the truckload of goodies."

"Okay?"

"The only thing was, he demanded that the missing items be returned personally by Tofer. If Sirel did that, he knew it would be good as sentencing Tofer to death."

"What did he do?"

"A rat is at its most dangerous when cornered. Sirel offered Tofer a sixty-forty chance of survival. He was to take all the missing items back to Zdanov, except for the two most important diadems."

"Why keep those?"

"One diadem was for Irma, to keep her on board. The other he kept for himself, for insurance and as a bargaining counter."

"And if Tofer refused?"

"His alternative was to go into a room with Vladi and a group of friends—to play a special game of Russian roulette."

I didn't look at Vladi. The cold glint in Toivo's eyes told me everything.

"What happened?"

"Tofer went, sweating blood and shit. He knew there was no escape. But that rat's brain of his had already worked out a survival plan."

He and Vladi exchanged glances, and there was a momentary silence.

"What happened?"

It was Vladi who answered, his mouth still looking curiously stiff.

"I came out of the swamps one fine, misty morning to find Tofer nailed to a tree."

I found myself recoiling. Toivo studied me in the mirror.

"Not easy to kill off something like Tofer," he remarked softly.

"Tofer had done a deal with Zdanov," said Vladi. "He told him about the gold. It bought him his life. He had a new proposal for Sirel from Zdanov. Zdanov would accept half of the gold as compensation for the items still missing from the treasure."

He paused, and they both looked at me.

"So?"

"So negotiations began. Sirel countered the proposal by offering one-quarter of the gold, providing it came out of Tofer's share."

"That put Tofer and Irma in a pretty pickle," said Toivo with evident relish. "After a lot of agonising, she agreed to give up her diadem. Zdanov got one more diadem back, and Irma got to share Tofer's share of the gold."

"That still leaves one piece missing from the treasure—the diadem Sirel held on to."

"That's right," said Toivo.

"Don't forget," murmured Vladi, "that Zdanov is a big greedy rat who wanted more."

"A big greedy rat," added Toivo, "whose pride has been scratched."

"So, of course, it didn't end there?"

"No, it didn't end there." Toivo shook his head emphatically.

Sirel's men got to the sawmill as fast as they could. The six men he had left on guard were Winter War veterans. They found them all later up in the loft, their throats cut, clearly the work of Zdanov's paratroop regiment specialists. The sawmill bristled with paras and NKVD sharpshooters.

Zdanov had taken the extra precaution of snatching a group of mothers and their children from the school in the local village. These he was holding as hostages in an adjoining building. Among the women was the young wife of local postman Vladi Lepp.

The siege went on for three days. Zdanov could not get the gold out; Sirel could not get in. The stalemate ended when Zdanov ordered the first of the mothers to be sent out. As she started to run, a shot rang out, and she fell dead in the snow. It was Vladi's wife. Vladi went berserk, and the partisans had to hold him down, or he would have run to his death.

Just before dawn the next morning, the partisans stormed the building where the women and children were being held. The rescue failed, and in the process, Sirel was captured.

Zdanov had him tied to the bench on which the circular saw was mounted. As the saw started to spin, a single shot rang out. A window shattered, and the Russians saw Zdanov collapse, blood pumping from his neck.

The Russians fought their way out of the sawmill, taking Zdanov with them. As they retreated, they blew up the building where the women and children were, including Vladi's two little boys.

Toivo halted his narrative and glanced at me. I could think of nothing to say at first.

"So," I said, addressing Toivo, "that's when you shot Zdanov?"

Toivo nodded solemnly and just glanced at me.

"He was the best shot in the whole region," said Vladi with a quiet pride.

"I was up in the signal box above the railway line that ran past. It was the luck of the devil that Zdanov moved when he did, or I'd have shattered his skull like a melon."

"What happened to Sirel?"

"The saw chopped off his left hand."

"What?"

Toivo considered me gravely in the mirror.

"Next time you see him," he said soberly, "look at his left hand. It's a what-you-call-it . . . prosthesis."

I was taken aback. I had always considered myself to be observant. We were silent for a while.

"It was only when all that was over," murmured Toivo, "that Vladi discovered that it was Tofer who had murdered his father and brother at the sawmill."

He glanced at me. I felt unable to look at Vladi or to ask him anything. There was a tense silence.

"What happened to the gold?"

"We took it down to Aleks's home place in the Viljandi swamps," said Vladi.

Neither of them seemed to want to add anything to that, and we all became thoughtful.

"The gold," said Toivo, when I thought the subject had been forgotten, "is quite a different story."

He checked the mirror to see if I was interested.

"Yes?"

He seemed to be marshalling the facts in his head.

"It all started when Hans Kersting was working at the new Gehlen Bureau quarters at Pullach in Bavaria."

"Okay."

"One day," interpolated Vladi, "he gets wind of this CIA scheme to activate their 'werewolf' radio contact in Estonia. Aleks Kallas was supposedly the contact, but he had automatically passed the responsibility on to Sirel, because he was the real connection with Kersting."

"Okay."

"There was this fast-talking, wheeler-dealer CIA character called William Smith O'Brien that Kersting put in contact with Sirel."

He paused to smile cynically. I could see that Toivo had picked up the mood.

"This smooth-talking Yank," said Toivo, "has a sweet, sweet scheme to run guns into Estonia. Object of the exercise? To activate them there partisans, with a view to knocking the old Russkies up a bit. It's Cold War time, see?"

"But the partisans were already armed and active!"

"Sure they were!" agreed Vladi. "But the chaps in Britain's SIS were running their famous Operation Jungle in the very same arena, using that nasty specimen, former Nazi Alfons Rebane."

"Okay."

"O'Brien had hinted that certain parties—with connections in the American Jewish Congress—might be grateful, in a financial sense, if someone were to bump off Rebane. Kersting contacted Sirel. Sirel said that he would be pleased to assist"

"In return," said Toivo, "Sirel wanted O'Brien to arrange to get the gold and the truckload of goodies out of Estonia. He wanted it routed through Germany and into Switzerland. Kersting agreed to fix the paperwork in return a little slice of the proceeds."

I looked from one to the other. Grudging admiration congealed on their faces.

"So what happened?"

"Our daredevil Pimpernel," said Toivo, "ex-Nazi Rebane, is heading for the Estonian coast in a speedboat when, inexplicably, he runs into a KGB trap—"

"But he escapes by the skin of his teeth," said Vladi.

"What about the gold and the truckload of stuff?"

Vladi and Toivo exchanged one of their quick-touch looks. Vladi heaved a deep sigh and assumed a sober expression.

"First," he said, "the gold and the other stuff had to be gotten to the coast by the partisans. Aleks Kallas and Johann Semmal were in charge of that part."

He paused.

"What is it you don't want to tell me?" I asked.

They exchanged looks again, but I noticed that they were avoiding eye contact with me. Toivo seemed to be secretly amused. After a long pause, he said, "The partisans—the 'Forest Brothers'—understood that they were going to get arms, explosives, timers, et cetera—all the stuff they needed to fight a real war, in exchange for the gold and the other stuff."

"Were they going to get these arms?"

"Oh yes, they were. More than they bargained for, only not in exchange for the gold."

"What do you mean?"

"The CIA was going to give them to them anyway."

"What about the gold?"

"The gold," said Vladi soberly, "and the paintings, and the jewellery, and the silver all ended up in a very respectable establishment in Switzerland."

I stared at him. He returned the look with interest.

"Who benefited from that?"

"With the proceeds, Sirel and O'Brien went into business together in the arms trade. Aleks Kallas took his share to Ireland and set up a boat-repair yard with it. Kersting gave up his job in the 'Bureau,' and moved to Ireland too. He went into the antiques business."

Toivo wasn't saying anything, but he kept glancing in the mirror.

"What about Tofer? Did he get his share of the gold?"

Toivo heaved a deep sigh before answering

"He got his share. He and Irma headed off for Argentina in order to become serious millionaires. They blew the lot in about twelve months and then came back with just enough to start up their ski school in Austria."

Clearly, that gave him a certain satisfaction.

"What about Johann Semmal and Zdanov?"

"Johann Semmal," answered Vladi, "was shot dead by Russian paratroopers in Viljandi Forest in 1956."

"Zdanov," said Toivo, "survived every shift in power during Stalin's time. And later, through the Kruschev, Breznev, Yeltsin, and Gorbachev eras, he climbed steadily all the time up through the party organization."

We thought about that for a while.

"What did Sirel do with the diadem that he held on to?"

"Well now," said Vladi soberly, "maybe you should ask Sirel himself that question." Toivo was nodding away in agreement.

We were approaching Heathrow. The two cars were still behind.

"Why are the three cars going to the airport?"

"We're going to Ireland, John," said Toivo, "to your part of the country."

The ironic expression was there again. I was taken aback.

"Why?"

"Angela's going to visit her great-aunt Hilge on the island for a while," said Vladi.

His expression was serious, apart from the glint in his eyes.

"There must be at least seven men between the two cars."

Vladi nodded solemnly as if seriously considering the implications of what I had said.

"They've booked a winter group holiday at a small lakeside hotel."

"They've booked a what?"

They were avoiding eye contact with me again. Eventually, Toivo answered, eyes glimmering as if having trouble containing the internal laughter.

"They're on a shooting holiday. They'll be out on the lake mostly."

They both gazed studiously away from me. I felt certain it was a leg-pull.

Toivo glanced at me once or twice, sobered up, and said seriously, "They're all carrying genuine Italian passports and cards showing membership of a game-shooting club near Bergamo."

A surreal atmosphere had suddenly been generated. I decided just to play along.

"Can any of them speak Italian?"

"One of them can—and Bergamasco."

Vladi was clearly not going to comment.

"Who's looking after Hilge now?"

"Habermel is."

"You mean by himself?"

"He's not by himself."

"Oleksandr here," said Vladi, "is going to join him. By the way, this is Oleksandr."

He said something in Russian to the big man in the front passenger seat. The big man turned around heavily and gazed at me. He had thick glasses that made his eyes look like pebbles. He extended his left hand and briefly grabbed the tops of my fingers.

"I am Oleksandr Yelahin," he said in heavily accented German. "We can speak in German."

Then he turned back and said no more. In spite of his size, he looked like a professor.

"What exactly does Oleksandr do?" I asked.

Vladi seemed to hesitate and then met Toivo's gaze in the mirror.

"He's a contract killer. The best in the business."

The silence in the car suddenly seemed to become more intense.

"And he's working for Sirel?"

Vladi took his time as if carefully choosing his words.

"Oleksandr was a top KGB operative. He ran Zdanov's operation in Kiev."

"What do you mean by 'operation'?"

"I mean operations, rackets—whatever! Oleksandr had a son. Zdanov was feeding his drug habit and encouraging his homosexual proclivities."

"Why?"

"It's simple. Zdanov himself is homosexual."

"So?"

"The son committed suicide. Oleksandr has sworn to kill Zdanov."

Toivo's eyes were like stones, staring straight ahead. We all fell silent.

"Is Habermel what he says he is—a businessman in Israel?"

Vladi seemed more reluctant to speak.

"He is now. Back in 1951, he was inducted into the Mossad's Collections Department. Later, he was sent into Syria with Eli

Cohen, the spy who infiltrated the Syrian government during the 1960s. Cohen was arrested and executed. Habermel—or Ari Yakhin, as he then was—got out just in time. He retired; went into the citrus fruit business."

There was another long, thoughtful silence.

"You ever ask yourself, John," murmured Toivo, "why your police were so interested in watching that island Hilge lives on?"

"They told me why. In any case, they had to check out Hans's suicide."

Vladi and Toivo looked hard at each other in the mirror.

"He didn't commit suicide," rasped Vladi. There was an edge of contempt in his voice.

"Tofer and his son got him," said Toivo grimly, "and made it look like he snuffed himself."

He stared at me with that blank expression he could instantly assume.

෨෩෨

Chapter 6

ᏯᏯᏯᏯ

MARTIN CUSACK HAD insisted on meeting in the forest car park. On the phone, he had seemed reluctant to talk, and now I got the impression that he was wary. We were sitting in my car.

"Was there something you wanted to tell me, John, in connection with Hans's death?"

"I don't mind telling you anything I know, Martin, but first, would you mind telling me what the result of the autopsy was?"

He stared at me and said dryly, "Hans died as a result of gunshot wounds to the head, from his own shotgun."

"So it was suicide?"

He didn't answer. He was watching a car that had driven into the far end of the car park, crunching softly over the gravel. We both watched to see who it was. It was a local man, a retired shopkeeper. The dog jumped out as soon the door opened and started barking excitedly as the owner slowly extricated himself.

"This is confidential," said the policeman as he watched the man locking his car.

"Okay!"

"Hans's doctor had him on antidepressants for the last year."

"What about all the whiskey bottles?"

"He wasn't supposed to be drinking at all."

"So it was definitely suicide?"

"Of course it was! What else would it be?"

"And that's why all the Guards were out there? Why they'd been watching the place for weeks? Why his phone was tapped?"

Martin Cusack put his hand on the door handle as if prepared to leave. He turned and said, in his official manner, "This is now an official investigation. I'm not at liberty to divulge—"

"Martin, we've known each other for twenty years. I'm not a fool. These people really are friends of mine. Why is it official now? Was that the state pathologist who was on the island that day?"

He already had one foot out on the tarmac. He retracted it, pulled the door shut with an angry little gesture, and stared at me coldly.

"You ever breathe a word of—"

"I won't!"

"There was a lot of alcohol in Hans's system, some of it on the back of his collar."

"What does that mean?"

"It means he was lying on his back, on the floor, when that alcohol went into his system and that some of it spilled."

"Go on."

"There were marks on his wrists, which could be—*could be*—consistent with being tied, possibly to a chair—"

"Martin, who do you suspect? Because clearly you know that this was murder."

Martin heaved a deep sigh and considered me as if trying to decide something. Having decided, he resumed.

"There were two men in a boat who'd been hanging around the place for a few days. They seemed to be fishing. Turns out they were foreigners, staying at the Lakeside Hotel."

"So?"

"We checked them out. They had Italian passports. The hotel owner was puzzled by that because he heard them speaking German together."

"So what?"

"The hotel owner had the wit to write down the passport numbers. We checked with the Italian police. The passports were genuine. Addresses in Alto Adige—or South Tyrol—where the population is German-speaking."

"Okay."

"One week later, we heard from the Italian police again. The passports were genuine but had been lost or more likely stolen. By that time, the two 'Italians' had disappeared."

Toivo had advised me against making further visits to the island. It was clear that Sirel had made arrangements to protect Hilge and Angela without attracting attention.

"Just one thing I need an answer to," I said as we waited for our flight at Heathrow "Doesn't Hilge know that Hans was murdered?"

People and noise swirled around us like heavy seas. Our group was like a still centre. Toivo studied me as if working out the implications of what I had said.

"So far as Hilge is concerned, Hans killed himself. She needs to think that, you understand?"

I wanted to think about that, but he had moved on.

"There's just one more thing, John."

I noticed immediately that his voice had changed and that he had fixed me with a look.

"Yes?"

"When you go to Austria, Vladi and I will be lurking in the background."

"Think of us as your guardian angels," said Vladi with poker-faced humour.

"Sirel's orders," said Toivo dryly, in answer to my unspoken question.

"I have one last question."

"Okay."

"Did you get your share of gold?"

It instigated an exchange of looks.

"I consider that a very personal question, don't you, Vladi?"

"I do," he said, nodding emphatically, pretending to be offended.

"Sirel doesn't forget his friends," said Toivo soberly.

Salzburg, in Austria, where the mountains rise to some 3,000 metres, is where the serious skiers go. The end of February or March is the favourite season, when the skies are blue, the sun shines, and the freshly fallen *pulverschnee* is perfect in daytime temperatures of around minus ten degrees Celsius. From the airport in Vienna, however, we drove the two-hour journey to Steiermark, where the slopes peak at a more modest 2,000 metres. I had booked into a Pension in the village of Dorfl, where the garrulous Frau Schwolberger assured me that I would not get fifty metres up the mountain road to Herr Kastner's *schischule* next morning without fitting snow chains to the tyres of the car. Her daughter Aurelia took one look at me and decided that her brother Albert should help me put them on that evening while there was still light. I made no mention of Toivo or Vladi, who had made their own arrangements in a Gasthaus down the street.

No one could call her curious, Frau Schwolberger assured me, and she kept herself to herself, but she was wondering why I should go to a place like the Bergschloessl.

Herr Kastner of course was an expert skier, and his son Eberhard had won prizes, but they only ever took groups of schoolkids up there, beginners mostly. I assured her, in turn, that I was a tour operator from London, a former teacher, and that I had come to talk to Herr Kastner about precisely that kind of business. Oh, she had wondered about that, seeing as I had an Irish passport. There was something odd about Herr Kastner, she thought. Of course, it might be depression or the drink, she hinted darkly, as she took the hot bread out of the oven. Not that it was any of her business. As for that haughty German wife of his! It was clear that the Family Kastner, alias Tofer, was not exactly popular in the village.

A harsh wind threw snowflakes against the windshield the next morning as I slowly negotiated the mountain road. Around a bend, on the right, the Bergschloessl was suddenly on the skyline above the trees, stone base rising sharply from a rocky knoll, wood structure above. It was three storeys high, more like a tower, somehow harsh against the background of snow and forest. There was a flat clearing just below it, where a red, white, and blue touring coach stood, with engine idling. Fifty or sixty schoolkids milled around noisily, trying out their skis. The legend on the back of the coach told me that it was from Billingshurst in Sussex. The driver sat at the wheel, finishing a cigarette, his elbow out the window. He was listening, frowning in concentration, to the two men talking below. The stocky one with the blue anorak had his back to me. His right arm hung loosely, cupping a cigarette from the wind. He lifted it twice in quick succession, sucking in his cheeks as he pulled on it. Both times, he threw up his chin before releasing the smoke in a jet. He turned his head and stared briefly, absorbing details, as I switched off the engine. As soon as I saw the bony skull with the ski cap pulled tightly down and those eyes, I knew it was Tofer. There was something offhand, even casually contemptuous, in the way he had been listening to the tall Englishman's careful German. Now he rumbled some inaudible reply, turned abruptly, and walked away.

Tofer had to be in his seventies, but he walked like an athlete, giving slightly at the knees, as he crunched towards me across the snow. He had his hand extended, frowning slightly, as I got out.

"So," he growled, "you're the man Aleks sent?"

"That's right! I'm John."

The handshake was curt.

"Kastner," he said dryly, "or Tofer, if you prefer. You drink this hot red-wine piss the Austrians go in for?"

"In this cold, I'd drink anything that—"

"You call this cold?"

He had already started a fast swinging walk up towards the house, throwing the words over his shoulder. He stopped so suddenly that I almost collided with him.

"Suomussalmi!" he said, with a savage stare. "Now, *that* was cold."

Opinions vary widely concerning the precise weather conditions at Suomussalmi in central Finland on 29 December 1939. Some Russian generals have claimed temperatures of minus forty-four degrees Celsius with blizzard conditions and up to four feet of snow. What nobody disputes is that some of the most spectacular engagements of the Winter War took place there. When the battle was over, 28,000 of the 500,000 Russian troops were dead, 1,300 taken prisoner. Of the 100,000 Finns—including the special Estonian unit—900 had died. As they approached Suomussalmi that day, the Russians, with their heavy transports, tanks, and artillery, were strung out in a twenty-mile-long column back along the road. The onslaught by the highly mobile, mounted Finns and the Estonian unit on skis was so effective that Russian tank divisions broke away across the frozen lakes, only to disappear into holes blown in the ice in front of them. Aleks Kallas records finding reconnaissance pilots frozen into still life in the trees, the white mounds on the ground—sometimes with their throats cut—that had been Russian patrols.

"We came at those poor sods of Russkies," said Tofer, "out of the snowstorm like a bunch of fucking ghosts in white camouflage, Schmeissers hammering away. I saw field kitchens, transports, tanks, bodies—burning like torches. Screaming like stuck pigs, they were."

"How was that done?"

"How was—Molotov fucking cocktails, that's how! We invented the cocktail! You lit the fuse, you threw it into the truck, and voom! Up it went!"

"These Russian tanks, falling into holes in the ice—"

"That was Sirel's specialty. Some lads from the granite quarries were brought in to make these home-made bombs with dynamite."

"What about the Molotov cocktails?"

Tofer shrugged.

"We got 70,000 empty bottles from the State Liquor Board, added petrol and fuses." He was staring at me. "You want to make small talk out here while your balls freeze solid? Or maybe you'd prefer some warming liquid refreshment inside?"

"Let's go inside!" I shouted into the wind.

Tofer shrugged out of his ski jacket, kicked off his boots, and shouted something in through a door. A female voice called something back from a far room. Tofer produced a strange, crooked little grin. His nose seemed to move slightly to one side as he did. It had been broken a few times. He had a gold cap on one front tooth.

"Hot wine isn't ready yet," he told me as if confidentially, "but never fear!"

He was reaching up, opening a cupboard door. He took down a bottle of colourless liquid.

"We have this!" he exclaimed. He held up the bottle, with a peculiar look of satisfaction.

The eyes were brown, hard, hooded, and slightly protuberant. There seemed to be no life in them as if a nerve behind had been severed.

"It's the local schnapps," he explained as if humouring me. "Wanna try it?"

"Don't mind if I do."

The act of drinking together seemed to improve Tofer's manners. He had slowed down, gone into contemplative mode, as if the fiery liquid had brought out another side of his character.

"So," he said quietly "Aleks, finally, is dead?"

I nodded.

"He died just over five years ago."

I had explained everything to Irma over the phone the previous week. Tofer wasn't there. She had said that I should come anyway since he had said he'd see me. Tofer had gone into a strange catatonic stillness, staring at the floor, the hooded eyelids unblinking.

"He was the most brilliant commander I ever knew!" he exclaimed, his voice curiously dry and cracked. He cleared his throat and looked at me. "Germans gave him the Iron Cross after nine months on the Russian Front. Did you know that?" he demanded.

I nodded.

"What we did under Aleks," he asserted aggressively, "was *unique*. Don't forget that!"

I nodded again.

He was deeply thoughtful for a moment then said quietly, "I said I'd help you. What do you want to know?"

"Tell me about you and Sirel."

"What about Sirel?" he demanded.

"According to Aleks, you, Corporal Eduard Poom, and Sirel joined the SS in Finland in June 1940—"

"Sure we did, but not together, not at the same time."

"What happened exactly?"

"Me and Poom got picked up by Zdanov's NKVD the night Sirel took off."

"Why?"

"'Detained for questioning,' as these dickheads so nicely put it.; in other words, kick you shitless first, questions second."

"Was there a specific reason for the arrest?"

"There was an *official* reason. Zdanov has this long list of suspects who had gone to Finland to fight the Winter War."

"What was the unofficial reason?"

Tofer produced his disconcerting grin.

"Now, that's a little more complicated."

The Molotov-Ribbentrop Pact may have been a ploy by Hitler to keep Stalin happy until the former was ready to attack Russia. Nevertheless, Stalin dutifully fulfilled his side of the bargain by supplying Germany with enormous quantities of food. One of the results of this was an acute food shortage in Russia itself. When the Russians invaded Estonia in June 1940, the militia immediately began scouring the countryside with the same objective but not quite the same result. The requisitioning in Estonia created a black market in foodstuffs and alcohol which, between June 1940 and June 1941, generated a huge illicit income for some local militia chiefs and their racketeering contacts in the cities. Some of the latter were even supplying sources in Russia.

According to Aleks Kallas, Andrei Ivanovitch Zdanov, born into the abysmal poverty of a Russian-speaking millworker's family in the industrial city of Narva in 1910, had three aims in life. The first was to acquire power by any means. This would afford him the opportunity to achieve his second aim, the acquisition of money, which would buy him his third aim, freedom, as he understood it.

Also according to Aleks, the train, which had borne the Estonian government eastward, was barely out of sight when Zdanov began scanning the list of Winter War suspects. Well down on that list, apparently, he saw a name he knew—that of Aarand Tofer, the snotty-nosed fifteen-year-old tough from the backstreets of Narva, who had been jailed with him in Tallinn on a charge of grievous bodily harm.

"Zdanov had been in jail?"

"Sure, early in his career—for his Communist Party activities."

"What did he want from you?"

"Well, now," said Tofer, rasping a square, meaty hand over his chin as if to hide his sly expression, "me and Poom have this nice little enterprise established, with the aim of supplying some friends of mine in Narva, whose purpose it was to prevent famine in Russia."

He paused so that I could work out the implications.

"So," I said, "Zdanov arrests you and Poom because he wants a piece of the action?"

"Piece of the action!" echoed Tofer. He stared at me with undisguised contempt. "He wanted to take over our little enterprise, lock, stock, and barrel."

"So?"

"This is why he interviews us. This is why I hear Poom screaming his guts out in the cell next to mine. I calculate that our number is up when we get this lucky break."

"How do you mean?"

"Just as a matter of interest—incidentally, you might say—Zdanov wants to know why Poom and I are making a break for Finland instead of Sweden. So Poom tells him about the secret SS training in Finland."

"Yes?"

"That turned out to be a lucky move, because Zdanov is very, very interested in this information."

"So?"

"So Poom and I are released—on one condition! That we report back to Zdanov, in the greatest detail, on everything the Germans get up to in Finland."

"What about the black market racket?"

"We're promised our place in that little enterprise, soon as we get back."

"Did you report everything to Zdanov?"

"Not . . . everything," he said carefully.

"Then Sirel, Poom, and you were parachuted back into Estonia in June 1941 as part of the German invasion?"

"That's right."

That gave me plenty to think about.

"Aleks said that you and Poom applied for special leave of absence in May 1942 in order to go to Finland to attend some kind of SS ceremony?"

"That's right, but not Sirel."

"What do you mean?"

"Sirel went too, but he didn't need anyone's permission. He came and went as he pleased."

"Why was that?"

"He was working for German Intelligence."

"Did you know that at the time?"

"No, I didn't."

"What was so important about this SS ceremony?"

"Two things. First, we were going to get our commissions. Second, Hitler himself was going to be there."

"Hitler!"

I stared at him. My expression elicited the crooked grin again. My brain was racing, juggling facts and dates.

"Where and when exactly was this?"

"It was 4 June 1942. It was right outside the private railway saloon carriage belonging to Marshal Mannerheim himself. Near a place called Imatra."

"But why was—"

"It was Mannerheim's seventy-fifth birthday—also the day he was made marshal of Finland, the only officer ever promoted to that rank. That was the real reason why Hitler was there."

"Tell me about Hitler."

To my surprise, Tofer began a strange, dry chuckling, shaking his head, remembering something.

"Hitler arrives in this Fw 200 Condor which nearly crashes into the chimney of Kaukopaa paper mill because of the low clouds—" He broke off to grin at me, and then resumed. "Finnish Army rules had to be broken in order to provide his men with some soothing alcohol. To help them recover from the fright they'd got."

His grin widened, and he just went on gazing at me. I was still digesting this unexpected twist to the story, questions vying with each other.

"So Sirel—"

"Sirel made Sturmbannführer. Poom, Scharführer. I made Hauptscharführer."

"I can hardly believe that all this stuff with Hitler really happened."

"Oh, it happened, all right," said a woman's voice behind me, and there she stood, holding a tray with steaming drinks on it. She put it down carefully on a table, straightened up unhurriedly and said, "Hitler himself officiated at the ceremony; shaking hands; saying a few words to each man, Marshal Mannerheim smiling over his shoulder. We have photographs somewhere."

She gave a tiny frown as if trying to remember where. The first thing I noticed about her was the very erect way she stood. She was slim, petite, and ageless. Cool, haughty, and aristocratic. The eyes were very steady and focused.

"I'm Irma, wife to this oaf who didn't think to make the introductions."

Tofer grinned somewhat sheepishly. It was clear that he adored her. An impression struck me like a film flashed on a wall—Tofer and Irma were not two people relating but two blind forces interacting. And that blind force, Tofer, was savagely murdering someone I had known—Hans Kersting.

Only seconds could have passed, because she was just turning her head, having addressed her remark reprovingly to Tofer, rather than to me.

"So," I said, "you were in Finland too?"

"Yes, I was."

The statement was cryptic, accompanied by a cool stare. It was an aristocratic device employed to keep people in their places or wrong-foot them if necessary.

"What was your reason for being there?"

Irma and Tofer exchanged amused glances.

"Why don't we have our drinks first, while they're still hot?"

She'd said it to dictate the pace, control the situation. There was silence while we sipped and Tofer slurped.

At length, she said, in that precise, cut-glass manner, "I was there because I was the official Abwehr contact with Finnish Intelligence."

I said nothing, remembering, with a certain satisfaction, Sirel's version of the same situation. She was watching me closely.

"Despite what Sirel may have told you, I was perfectly well aware of his *unofficial* contact with Finnish Intelligence—and Mannerheim himself—through the medium of the beautiful Ms Kaisa Jarvinen. Their relationship was hardly a secret."

"The relationship between—"

"Sirel and Kaisa Jarvinen. They were married in Mannerheim's little office in Mikkeli."

I felt the impact of that unexpected glimpse of Sirel's life, but perhaps perversely, I was determined not to pursue the subject with Irma.

"But you weren't based in Helsinki at that time. I mean, at the German Embassy."

"Berlin was my permanent base. I was on a training course in Helsinki when they told me Hitler was coming."

Irma seemed equally determined to give nothing away.

"I take it you knew Hitler personally?"

"I mixed with them all. Hitler, Göring, Ribbentrop. That little fart Goebbels."

"And you found that easy to do?"

Irma studied me with cool arrogance, drew a good, long breath up through thin nostrils, and said, "My family came to Estonia from Germany back in the thirteenth century. We had very large estates, which generations of drinking, gambling, and whoring males of the line had managed to reduce to a tiny estate and a very large house near Nomme, just before the Second World War. We were spoiled, overeducated, much travelled, and living in genteel poverty by the time the War broke out. In addition, we were all suffering in our different ways from crises of identity. When I attended a very expensive school in Hannover, they thought of me as Estonian. In Estonia, they thought of us as Baltic barons. In Berlin, however, I used my Baltic baroness trappings up to the hilt."

She gave a grim little smile. Tofer assumed a similar expression.

"So that's how you got to see the Trojan treasure at Cairnhall?"

"See the treasure!" she exclaimed in amusement to Tofer. He grinned knowingly. She studied me again, her manner patronizing.

"Reichsmarschall Hermann Göring was a fat, overgrown fart of a schoolboy, a transvestite. A ferocious snob, who had his so-called family crest stamped on everything, from silver-mounted corkscrews with stag-horn handles to God knows what. That hunting lodge of his was full of such junk."

"Did he keep the Trojan treasure there?"

"I don't know how it got there. But one evening, he was giving a rather special party."

She broke off to exchange a sly or knowing look with Tofer.

"Of course, there were special guests that evening, for whom he'd decided to provide some special entertainment."

She paused and gave me a strange, smug look.

"He decided to display the Trojan treasure?" I prompted.

She surprised me by laughing outright. As if on cue, Tofer slapped his thigh, either in amusement or satisfaction.

"In a manner of speaking, yes," she said, her eyes still brimming with amusement.

"Göring decided that this antique jewellery would be displayed to best advantage if I were to be adorned only with them, without the encumbrance of clothing."

"You were naked?"

"The guests that night thought that if Leni Riefenstahl could dance naked for Hitler, why shouldn't I for them?"

Her gaze was both amused and challenging. Suddenly, in one swift, fluid movement, she was on her feet, raising her arms in a graceful, flowing rhythm, and slowly, her hips gyrating seductively as she did so. The effect was so sensual that I forgot for a moment what age she was. Then she stood still and silent in the centre of the floor before beginning to execute a very different kind of dance.

It began with some rhythmic, march-like foot movements, her spine ramrod straight, her expression trance-like. Immediately, her arms snapped up and began to execute a series of movements, seemingly unrelated. To these were added separate head movements, also apparently unrelated, everything perfectly coordinated. I was struck by the precision, the sheer complexity, the simple other-worldly beauty. Most remarkable was the fluidity and lack of tension.

She came to a sudden stop and remained stock-still, arms aloft, one foot forward, her gaze angled upward at forty-five degrees. Then she quietly resumed her seat. It must have lasted twenty minutes.

Nobody spoke. They were both serious and still, whilst I was recovering from my astonishment. The dance had changed or moved something essential in Irma. It was as if a different person sat opposite. Gone was the aristocratic hauteur, the arrogance, the controlling factor. In their place was someone quiet, deeply contemplative, even gentle.

"What was that dance?"

"It's an ancient Greek temple dance, as old as the Eleusinian Mysteries."

"Is that what you did at Cairnhall?"

"Yes."

"Naked?"

She smiled gently.

"Not naked. We were just pulling your leg a little."

"Why would you do such a dance for those . . . for Göring and the others?"

"It was vanity on my part. They were so self-important, those swaggering Nazis. They wanted a female mannequin, preferably naked, to dance some provocative dance. They were jaded, depraved, corrupt, the nihilist society of 1920s and '30s Berlin, craving entertainment. Göring himself put that diadem on my forehead."

"What happened then?"

"I wanted to shock them. Show them another reality. Show them a mystery I knew them to be incapable of understanding."

"Apart from shocking them, was there any other reason for the dance?"

"When I was a young girl, I discovered that I have some kind of psychic gift, which is activated when I dance. I see things. I knew with certainty the moment that diadem was placed on my head that it was very ancient and very special."

"Where did you learn that particular dance?"

"It was taught to me by an aunt of mine, in France in 1938. She had been a student of Jaques-Dalcroze. Her husband Alexander, my uncle, was a painter. He knew Rilke and Kandinsky. He'd been at Hellerau. He'd died a few years previously, of course."

"So you were a dancer?"

"I was sent to France, when I was sixteen years old, to study dance. During my second year there, I was invited by my aunt and some friends, one weekend, to a large country house, to take part in an interesting experiment. They had invited this strange Russian man, who told me he had composed a piece of music especially for me. According to him, I had a rare psyche, susceptible to combinations of halftones. He told me that when a particular chord was struck, I would fall into a state of deep hypnosis."

"So?"

"That's exactly what happened. From the opening notes, I found myself listening intently. I was deeply moved. My aunt told me afterwards that, as soon as that chord was struck, my head fell back, and my body went completely limp."

"Do you remember anything of what happened while you were hypnotized?"

She looked at me as if surprised.

"Of course I do! We conducted the experiment several times. The Russian would put a question to me, concerning some remote period of history. I would immediately see a vivid, living scene, as in a cinema."

"How is this related to what took place at Cairnhall?"

"At Cairnhall that night, I realized that I might never have another opportunity to wear that jewellery or to discover the significance of the compelling feeling I was getting from it, particularly the diadem. On an impulse, I decided to go into the hypnotic trance, passing it off as a party trick."

"How—"

"The music the Russian had composed for me was indelibly printed on my mind. I wrote it down and instructed a Wehrmacht colonel to play it on the piano, having explained beforehand what would happen."

"What *did* happen?"

"As predicted, I fell into a trance. What I saw was a woman on the deck of a ship, her arm linked through the arm of a man who was clearly a king or prince. They were approaching land. People were pouring out of a city and running down to the shore, waving, and shouting with joy. The woman was wearing the diadem I wore. That woman was Helen of Troy."

I looked at her in astonishment. She looked quite serious, as did Tofer.

"But that's just a story, a legend, a—"

"Is it?"

On 30 May 1873, at seven o'clock in the morning, Heinrich Schliemann astonished the workmen at the Troy excavation by announcing a holiday. It was one of those stifling May mornings, the yellow dust already like a haze over the hot, dry plain. Close to the Scaean Gate, Schliemann had noticed "a container or implement of copper" about three feet long, peering through the dust and rubble. The workmen had noticed nothing, and the suspicious Amin Effendi, representative on site of the Turkish government, was nowhere to be seen. Schliemann instructed his equally astonished wife to shout *"Paidos! Paidos!"* (rest period) and waited until all the workmen had disappeared. He knew he'd made an important find.

As soon as he had carried it all, in his wife's shawl, back to the house, he locked the door and spread it all out on a rough wooden table, where it glowed with a wonderful reddish colour.

The treasure consisted of a copper cauldron, a copper shield, a silver vase, a copper vase, a gold flask and two gold cups, a gold sauceboat, and a cup of gold and silver alloy. There were three great silver vases, a silver goblet, seven copper daggers, six silver knife blades, thirteen copper lance heads. There was a fillet, 56 gold earrings, 8,750 gold rings and buttons. There were also axe heads of semiprecious stone.

Most astonishing were the two gold diadems, one of them consisting of ninety chains, forming an elaborate gold headdress, with leaf and flower pendants, and long tassels hanging down at the sides. This Schliemann placed on the head of his wife Sophia. He arranged necklace upon necklace around her neck. He put rings on her fingers. He fumbled and trembled with excitement. He had found the treasure of King Priam, secretly buried in the wall by the Scaean Gate, in the midst of the slaughter, whilst the whole city of Troy went up in flames.

Tofer was looking at his watch. He nodded to Irma. I looked at my own watch.

"This whole business about Helen of Troy—"

"Do you think Sirel was interested in doing business with Zdanov?" asked Irma.

"Sorry?"

Tofer leaned forward as if to explain something to me.

"I put Zdanov's proposition to Sirel—about staging an attack on the three trucks headed for Leningrad. He didn't want to know; laughed me out of it."

"Sirel got involved in that whole business," said Irma, "not because of Zdanov's truckloads of stolen art treasures but because of Priam's Treasure."

"Why?"

"Because Sirel saw exactly what I saw in my vision of Helen of Troy."

I looked from one to the other. Everything I had heard about them led me to believe that I was looking at nothing less than a pair of confident tricksters. Yet I felt compelled to hear whatever else they had to say.

"Sirel, in my opinion, is a hard-headed businessman. I can't imagine—"

"Sirel is psychic! I should know. I recognized it the moment Rebane first introduced us."

"What does that mean?"

"Sirel laughed at me in Sweden when I first mentioned a treasure buried under rubble in Berlin. But the psychic in him recognized the psychic in me. I managed to persuade him to take part in a little experiment before he went back into Estonia."

"What kind of experiment?"

Irma went still and gazed steadily at me as if looking for something. Her voice was different when she spoke.

"I helped him to see what I had seen—Helen entering Troy. You could see it too, if you were curious enough."

She said it in such a way that it seemed a challenge to my very manhood. They were both calmly gazing at me, Tofer's expression ironic.

"Well," said Irma quietly, "we have to move. Do things. If you're interested in what I suggested, come back around eight o'clock tonight."

Toivo sat in the passenger seat beside me. Vladi sat behind. Below us stretched the whole valley, the village of Dorfl nestling at the foot of the mountain. Lights were already going on as dusk set in.

I had expected Toivo to be scathing in his remarks and dismissive of everything I had related concerning the meeting with Irma and Tofer.

"It's for you to decide," he said quietly, "whether you go back or not. They've used drugs in the past. I'd strongly advise you not to get involved in anything like that."

"No fear of that!"

"On the plus side," said Vladi, "you'll probably get to meet Tofer Junior—young Eberhard."

ᠭᡍᡍᡉ

"This music," said Irma, "does not exist anywhere else. It's on this tape only and up here."

She tapped the side of her forehead. Her mood was solemn and purposeful.

"I have something else here," she added, producing a small, beautifully carved hardwood casket. It had a hinged lid, which she lifted. Inside, in neat, serried ranks were some dark-brown objects, suggestive of slim cigars but with tapers protruding.

"This is a special kind of incense, precious and rare, which will help you to see what I will see."

"Okay."

I had deep reservations about the whole enterprise, but my curiosity was stronger. Irma was moving around, calmly and quietly, arranging things.

"I'm going to light some candles," she murmured.

I had a curious impression of myself as a frightened child being soothed. The lights went off. It was so peaceful like a church, especially with the incense. We sat on very low stools with hassocks, in the centre of the floor, our legs underneath us in kneeling positions. We faced each other, almost touching, in a kind of triangle.

The music was strange, vaguely oriental, and rather sad. It did nothing for me. I liked the incense. It reminded me at first of good pipe tobacco, rather sweet. Gradually, I became aware of an acrid quality to it, which I experienced directly in my lungs. It was not unpleasant. It concentrated in my solar plexus as a cool sensation, reminiscent of the effects of menthol. I felt a strange numbness spreading through me. I noticed Irma's head collapsing, like that of a rag doll, against the pillar behind her. I felt quite indifferent. My head was completely empty of thoughts. I felt as if I were listening to my body.

There was a strange surging sensation beneath me, which I experienced in my stomach. I was on the deck of a small ship. I knew immediately that the woman before me was Helen. Great chestnut braids of hair were joined in a jewelled net at her waist. She was almost as tall as the king at her side, her figure proud and erect. There was something exquisitely graceful in her movement as she turned to speak to him. The profile was classically beautiful, but the real beauty was from within and in that grace. The heavy diadem seemed almost to be part of her and glowed about her as she moved. The voices of the people on the shore rose to a great, surging tide of joy.

The noise increased in volume, sucking me up into a black vortex, and suddenly I was in a different place. It was a great hall, and I was witnessing the slaughter of guests at a feast. Guttering sconces on stone walls moved the pillars about like shadows. On the floor, awash with blood and wine, a king lay dying. A mask of gold looked calmly upward from where his face should have been. A man and a woman came to watch him die. The man suddenly thrust a dagger into the side of the king's neck. The dying man rose a moment, eyes bulging, throwing his attacker aside. The knife stayed in his neck, and blood gushed out. He collapsed, beating the floor with his fists. A horrible groan came bubbling up through the blood in his mouth. The golden mask was on the floor. The dead man's face was Sirel's.

I came to and heard the horrible, bubbling groan coming from my own mouth.

The victorious King Agamemnon returned home to Mycenae after the sack of Troy, only to be murdered at a banquet at the instigation of his wife Clytemnestra and her lover Aegisthus. According to the historian Pausanias, writing in the second century AD, the murderous pair were thought unworthy to be buried within the city walls. Schliemann held a different view. But his real interest was to find the grave of Agamemnon, which he believed was within the citadel in the agora.

By October 1876, driving rain had turned the dust to mud in the agora. Fifteen feet down, Schliemann found the first funeral pyre, glinting with gold. This time, the Greek government was taking no chances with the wily archaeologist. The officials who followed him everywhere immediately ordered the workmen off the site and placed a ring of soldiers around the find.

Five shaft graves in all were found at Mycenae, the fourth one yielding more treasure than had been found at Troy. But Schliemann was not happy. He had not found the grave of Agamemnon.

He spent his last days on the site carefully re-examining the first tomb. Digging deeper, he found three more bodies. Two wore gold masks. There was still flesh adhering to one of the skulls. It had been squashed flat, and the nose was missing, but the teeth were perfectly preserved. He wore a gold breastplate, and gold leaves adorned his forehead, chest, and thighs. Schliemann, excited beyond measure, raised the golden mask to his lips and kissed it. He had found Agamemnon.

The eyes on the death mask stood out in strong relief. The thin lips were pursed in a mysterious smile below the warrior's moustache. People came from all over to see the body of the ancient hero, whose face had been so miraculously preserved. They had forgotten that Homer had depicted Agamemnon as insensitive, irrational, self-obsessed, and cruel, whose ghost, speaking to Odysseus, had reconstituted himself as homecoming hero. That did not in any way inhibit the enthusiasm of Schliemann, writing to the king of Greece in November that year:

> With extreme joy I announce to Your Majesty that I have discovered the tombs which tradition, echoed by Pausanias, has designated as the sepulchres of Agamemnon and his companions. In the tombs I found immense treasures of the most ancient objects of pure gold . . . I work only for the pure love of science. I give them intact to Greece . . .

I have gazed upon the face of Agamemnon.

The next thing I knew, I was on my hands and knees on the snow outside. Tofer had rubbed snow on my face and neck. As the cold seeped in through my hands and knees, the full awareness of my body began to come back to me.

Vladi and Toivo came out of nowhere. Tofer was thrown away from me, and I saw Toivo with both hands grasping a gun. Toivo pointed the gun straight at Tofer's chest. Tofer was slowly getting to his feet. He listened to the sharp instructions in Estonian and then slowly got down on his knees, his hands clasped over his head. Vladi was standing directly behind him. In one fluid movement, Vladi leaned forward and pressed a thumb hard into a point on the side of Tofer's neck. Tofer collapsed and stayed still. Then Irma was shouting angrily from the house. Vladi replied in like manner.

"Get in the car, John," said Toivo tersely. "I'll drive."

He was there before me, and I silently handed him the keys.

"It's very simple," said Toivo as we approached the airport. "The smoke you inhaled was hallucinogenic."

"What about the music?"

Toivo scoffed, "That was just the right kind of story to set you up!"

I wasn't satisfied with Toivo's answer this time, and he knew it. Vladi was in the back, listening without comment. I had related only the first part of what I had seen. I wanted to talk to Sirel himself about the second part.

"Why did you feel it necessary to snatch me like that?"

Toivo looked at me as if I were a bit slow. But it was Vladi who answered.

"Because Habermel was snatched two days ago while he was on some legal business in Dublin for Hilge.

"Snatched?"

"By Zdanov," said Toivo grimly. "We weren't taking any chances with you."

"How do you mean?"

"When people start getting snatched, it means the negotiations are achieving the requisite temperature."

"What will happen to Habermel?"

"To begin with, Sirel might get a little package in the post, with one of Habermel's fingers in it—"

"Shit! Are Angela and Hilge okay?"

"They're safe."

"Hilge," said Vladi, "isn't taking it very well."

✎

Chapter 7

𝕺𝕸𝕸𝕺

THE SHELBOURNE HOTEL in Dublin has seen many changes since it opened its doors in 1824. The bronze slave girls, however, Nubian in aspect and art nouveau in design, still hold their torches aloft at the front door, one of the touches which help preserve the essential quality of the place. The Dickensian commissionaire, on the other hand, is more likely nowadays to be hailing taxis for Hollywood glitterati rather than for princes or famous writers.

Sirel was over by the windows in the Lord Mayor's Lounge, a study in still life. He was watching a group of people entering through the other archway. With the exception of one dominant Irish voice, they were clearly Americans. Sirel was reaching for the coffee pot, when he froze, staring at me. Then he was smiling, waving me in.

Sirel poured us both some coffee. He had gone through the preliminaries with attentive politeness.

"Trip to Austria go all right?" he asked casually.

"It was . . . interesting. I have lots of questions."

"They'll have to wait, I'm afraid."

He suddenly looked strained and preoccupied.

"How is Habermel?"

"He's going to be okay."

"How do you know?"

"We have as our guest," he said with cold cynicism, "a good friend Zdanov's."

"Who's that?"

"The great love of Zdanov's life—Peter Bremer. Nobody need lose any fingers."

"How did you manage to get hold of him?"

Sirel drew a deep breath, went completely still, and gazed steadily over at the group of Americans. They had settled down under the dark, varnished painting opposite the windows. There was a sudden outbreak of restrained laughter, and the Irishman became the focus of their attention. From that moment, he began to address them in low, persuasive tones.

"I sold this famous Trojan diadem," said Sirel, "to a colleague of mine in the arms trade, in Geneva. Understandably, he didn't want to sell it back to me."

"That's what's holding up the negotiations with Zdanov?"

He nodded briefly.

"So desperate measures, as one is entitled to say, were called for."

I was glad this time to see the ironic expression, somewhat wan, back in place.

"What did you do?"

"I called in a favour from an old friend of mine, former client—a Greek shipping magnate. He has, among his many possessions, his very own art thief."

He paused to study my expression.

"It sounds like a dangerous enterprise to steal from someone in the arms trade, especially a former colleague."

"It also happens that he's a friend. I flew in the best goldsmith in England, who spent quite some time making a replica of the Trojan diadem."

"Wouldn't Zdanov—or his experts—spot a forgery straight away?"

"They might, if they were the best in the world. And if they were looking for a forgery."

"How do you mean?"

"My friend's art thief, a Frenchman, freelances in his spare time. He thinks my friend doesn't know. He's done several big jobs on the side for Zdanov."

"You mean he did a deal with Zdanov?"

"He thought he was working for the Greek. Zdanov maintains a permanent presence in Zurich, in the person of his lover, Peter Bremer. It was no surprise to us when Bremer turned up—with a reception committee—to meet the Frenchman, who was on his way to the airport after the removal of the forgery from my friend's house, of course."

"And that's when you snatched Bremer?"

He nodded briefly as before. He was gazing over at the American group again. Nodding in their direction, he said ironically, as if to explain his interest, "Those gentlemen are prime specimens of the bloodstock sales breed—from Kentucky, US of A. Talking—or rather, listening to—the brother of one of your great Irish racehorse trainers."

I looked over and recognized a famous face.

"What happened to the forgery?"

"I have it."

"What about negotiations with Zdanov?"

He paused to gaze at me.

"They're still on track," he said with cool cynicism.

"What will happen now?"

"If Zdanov runs true to form, he will be beside himself with fury. He will not negotiate directly."

"What will he do?"

"He'll send a go-between."

He turned again towards the Americans. A tall, stately figure was walking in to join the group. It was more like making an entrance. His expensive western suit was not at all at odds with the formal Muslim headdress. He immediately became the focus of attention.

Some of the Americans rose to shake his hand, eager to do so. The Irishman was loudest in his greetings. He wasn't going to give up being the centre of attention that easily.

The Arab had spotted Sirel straight away. As soon as he could decently disengage, he turned towards Sirel and dipped his head towards him—moving from the waist in a kind of slow, silent obeisance. There wasn't a hint of humility in it. There was, rather, a touch of subtle irony.

Without moving from his seat, Sirel executed a miniature version in reply, moving from the base of his neck. The touch of irony was just the same.

The Americans had watched the proceedings as if they were at a play—the Irishman seemed to nod vaguely towards Sirel—and then they all homed in on the Arab again. Apart from occasional, oblique glances, Sirel and the Arab ignored each other from that point on.

"Who is he?"

Sirel sniffed as if in distaste.

"It has not been confirmed, but my educated guess is that *that* is our go-between."

"I take it you know him?"

"He's Saudi, an arms dealer. Anything from handguns to tanks."

He examined the expression on my face.

"He's not in Ireland to do business with your nationalist patriots."

"So what's he here for?"

Sirel paused to brush some invisible crumbs from his knees, a little frown creasing between his brows. His left hand looked so real.

"Apart from coming to visit his trainer at a well-known establishment down in County Tipperary, I imagine he's taking time out to oblige an important colleague."

I glanced over. The Saudi seemed the only free agent in the captive audience. His cunning, liquid eyes roamed restlessly, registering and collating incoming intelligence.

"But why the personal interest in this Saudi?"

Sirel examined me as if trying to decide something.

116

"It's because he reminds me of someone."

"He reminds you of . . . ?"

"Me!"

"Sorry?"

He gazed over at the group a moment, immobile, lost in thought.

"What are you thinking about right now?"

"About a man's life."

"Which man?"

"Konstantin Päts. He was a good man. And I sent him out to his death."

His face had acquired a blotchy, yellowish tinge. His intensity reminded me, once again, of Hilge.

The Alexander Nevsky Cathedral, opposite government buildings, is close to the summit of the great rock, which dominates Tallinn's skyline. Around midnight on 19 June 1940, journalist Peeter Sirel met the exhausted President Konstantin Päts there. Sirel was a member of a prominent family which was close to Päts. He was the confidant of Mannerheim of Finland, a discreet conduit between the two leaders—a man that Päts could trust, away from the conniving politicians in the chamber; away from the eavesdroppers, the Nazi sympathizers, and the Communist collaborators. He needed independent advice, an alternative viewpoint.

Candles guttered, glinting on old gold. Whispered prayers crept around the high stone walls as Päts knelt before the iconostasis.

Sirel advised him to sign the document he was being pressured to sign. It would prevent further shedding of Estonian blood. The document would give legal effect to the puppet government to be installed by Moscow, following the demise of his own government. The "demise" had been planned well in advance. Signing that document would seal Päts's own fate. What Päts could not have known was that Sirel had been promised a ministry in the government in exile, on the strength of his success in persuading Päts to sign. The next day, 20 June, almost the entire Estonian government was deported.

I stared at Sirel in disbelief.

"You mean you betrayed Päts?"

"Yes."

"Why?"

"Power! Everyone seeks it, consciously or unconsciously. The yogi, the fakir, the monk, all seek power over themselves. All politicians, all ambitious men, all men in public life—forget about the so-called idealists and altruists—all seek power over other people. We accept this real abnormality as the norm. In fact, it's a form of lunacy. It is in this environment that the lunatic most typically grows and develops. He values fame or power but puts no value on his fellow human beings. His ruthlessness stems from extreme selfishness and indifference."

We were silent for a while.

"What happened to Päts?"

"Died in the Kazan psychiatric prison hospital in 1956."

I suddenly had that vision again of the lake in Viljandi, Estonia, 1956, and the figure of Johann Semmal running towards it, the Russian paratroopers coming out of the trees, automatic weapons stuttering. Then Johann's body is shredding obscenely, the startled birds rising in clouds off the water behind, raucous in fright.

"How did he—"

"My brother Sasha died on 15 May the same year, by lethal injection, in Ward 6 of the same hospital. The TASS news agency reported that he had confessed to a number of war crimes."

"But that's impossible."

"Not if you've first been rendered unconscious with a hefty dose of sodium pentothal and then injected with Benzedrine to revive you. You'd believe anything. Confess to anything."

After the war, President Harry Truman was faced with the decision to force Switzerland to release Jewish assets. The Swiss banks and insurance companies were demanding that the heirs of concentration camp victims produce death certificates to prove that the depositors were indeed dead. This was the bind that Hilge Kersting had found herself in.

Realpolitik at the state department, however, argued that undue pressure from the US could drive Switzerland into the Soviet Union's sphere of influence. This was not implausible at the end of the Second World War, when most of central, and all of Eastern Europe, was falling to Communism. Later, the Americans' need of Swiss help in finding drug traffickers and money launderers maintained the stalemate.

The Swiss Bankers' Association, representing sixty-seven banks, would later publish a register of some 2,000 "dormant" accounts, with assets totalling some $44 m. The register did not allay suspicions. It was seen by many as an admission of past deceit. Worse, many high profile Holocaust survivors discovered that records of accounts, which they knew to exist, had simply been erased.

It was in this climate that Sirel's team of lawyers, working out of the Hotel St Gottard on the Bahnhofstrasse, began to press their case with the Swisse-Francaise Bank on the same street in Zurich. The bank was adamant, from the start, that only a certificate proving that her brother was dead could release Hilge's money. Her title documents were otherwise useless.

"So you can appreciate why we must negotiate with Zdanov."

"Yes, but why Zdanov?"

"It was Zdanov who ordered Sasha's arrest. Zdanov's NKVD who put Konstantin Päts in a car—the morning after the Estonian Government was deported—and drove him straight to Kazan. Zdanov who kept my brother alive until he discovered that the Swiss bank needed only a death certificate to release the equivalent of some £4 m. sterling. It was a situation he considered to be negotiable, to say the least. It was exactly the leverage he needed to recover the Trojan diadem."

"Not to mention his pride."

"Yes, that also."

The famous trainer's brother was still talking in low, urgent or persuasive tones. The Americans listened with rapt attention, nodding or delivering themselves of brief, affirmative remarks. Only the Saudi seemed immune.

"How did you manage to get a truckload of works of art and a consignment of gold into Switzerland?"

Sirel stared at me blankly a moment as if he had no idea what I was talking about. Then he smiled. Everything in him seemed to relax, and he was his old, ironic self.

"The Hotel St Gottard on the Bahnhofstrasse in Zurich is a venerable and most convenient institution. Do you know it?"

I shook my head.

"I chose it as my base, because in the very same street were two banking institutions with which I was destined to have many dealings—the bank where Hilge's money was and the Union Bank of Switzerland."

He paused to gaze at me.

"Is that where you put the gold and the other stuff?"

"It wasn't quite as straightforward as that."

Switzerland, in March 1947, immediately appealed to Sirel. It wasn't just the cleanliness, the orderliness, the clean air, or the mountains. It was the dull, prosaic normality, the absence of war, the focus on money, and the material things in life.

On his first Monday in Zurich, accompanied by CIA operative William Smith O'Brien, he called to the Panamanian consulate. O'Brien's specialization seemed to be getting things into and out of countries. As he had explained it to Sirel, the smart thing to do was to go through all the correct legal procedures. With the consul general's help, a down payment in cash, and a commitment to pay an annual fee, they acquired a ready-made, legally constituted company, registered in Panama. The package included a set of Panamanian directors, bearer shares constituting their legal title to the company, a minute book, and a document of procuration, which enabled them or persons designated by them to act on behalf of the company. The company could do whatever they wanted it to do, be it diamond mining or manufacturing shoes. It was registered as Norfax SPA.

From the consulate, they proceeded to the Union Bank of Switzerland. Having presented the bearer shares and documents of registration, they opened a company account and lodged a dollar draft provided by O'Brien. Then they rented, in the name of the company, a large safe-deposit box in which was lodged the foundation documents of Norfax SPA and a golden diadem from ancient Troy.

The bank was reluctant to recommend a lawyer to them, but considering they were new and potentially important clients, they bent the rules a little and recommended one Alois Zysset, a former lecturer in jurisprudence.

The arms-dealing side of the Norfax SPA enterprise was set up in Geneva. The year 1947 was a good year to get started, and O'Brien had the know-how and contacts. Some forty years later, after the Cold War, vast arsenals of NATO and Warsaw Pact weapons were legally and illegally finding their way to areas of tension. By 1991, this trade was generating about $22 b. NATO weapons were going to Greece and Turkey. Warsaw Pact weapons to Afghanistan, former Yugoslavia, Tajikstan, and other former Soviet republics. The biggest suppliers were still the US and the USSR. The biggest market was still the Middle East. Sirel and O'Brien sold NATO weapons; Zdanov sold Warsaw Pact stock. His representative in Geneva was Peter Bremer, formerly of BOSS, South African Intelligence, a psychotic personality that the South Africans were pleased to get rid of.

಄ಮಾಲಿ

"Why was it important to get a lawyer recommended by the bank?"

Sirel gazed at me as if pleased with my perspicacity.

"Secrecy is Switzerland's most valuable asset. There is a long and immensely profitable tradition of traffic across her frontiers. The Swiss government does not question how the stuff gets there. They will respond reluctantly to official representations about criminal activities, but they refuse absolutely to administer the fiscal or customs regulations of neighbouring countries."

"The Russians were unlikely to try claiming back stuff they'd stolen themselves elsewhere?"

"It has been calculated that, during the Second World War, some 330 tonnes of gold were stolen by the Nazis from occupied countries. It's thought that Switzerland handled about seventy-six per cent of all Nazi business, and much of it was transacted in gold." He paused to look at me. "To answer your question, in Switzerland, legal privilege between lawyer and client is absolute—including foreign clients like us. The introduction from the bank, in addition to a retainer of 10,000 Swiss francs, secured Alois Zysset as our personal lawyer and a colleague of his, Dr Heinz Liepert, as procurator for Norfax SPA."

"Why two lawyers?"

"It was to create a fiction whereby Norfax SPA would have an independent legal existence. Its ownership by us clouded in impenetrable secrecy. Its assets, possibly worth tens of millions of dollars, locked away in bank vaults."

"What about the diadem?"

"What about it?"

"You sold it to a colleague in the arms trade in Geneva. Didn't it mean anything to you personally?"

"Certainly," he said with cold cynicism. "It represented a business opportunity which I could not pass up. I knew that there were very wealthy people willing to pay enormous sums in order to procure something special, something no one else could possibly have had."

"Irma told me that you were psychic, that you had seen something in connection with the diadem that she had seen."

That certainly changed things. He gazed at me seriously, working out the implications.

"Did she persuade you to do a 'session' with her?"

"Yes."

"What did you see?"

I told him about the two visions I had seen. As I began to recount the details of witnessing the death of the king with the golden mask, he went into a catatonic stillness, and all the blood seemed to drain from his face. Discreet conversation washed all around us as if we were on an island.

"The incense she used was hallucinogenic, wasn't it?"

"That wouldn't matter. It was primarily for you. In the state you described, Irma can tell only the truth of what she sees."

"What does it all mean?"

Sirel turned as if in a daze to check on the Americans. They were still engrossed, and the Saudi looked bored.

"I was in London," began Sirel, his voice hoarse and strange, "in 1948. I was alone . . . in a suicidal state of mind. In the Russian baths, I met a man I'd met in Paris before the War. His name was Oswell, an industrialist. We got talking. To cut a long story short, this man immediately recognized my state of mind. We talked and talked for hours. He was so kind that in the end I almost wept like a child."

Sirel had never been a child. He had been embarrassed by children's games, as if he remembered himself as an adult from some previous life. It made him uncomfortable to feel that he was back again, an outsider looking on, unable to participate in a game which for him was meaningless and which made him suffer, because he did not know what the purpose was. The worst thing was the feeling of inevitability that the same mistakes would be made, the same sufferings gone through. He went through the motions, trying to understand. He realized that he was quite unable to believe in any of those things which those around him apparently believed in—ambition, careers, the accumulation of wealth, fame, prestige, love, and all the rest of it. He felt he could not begin any enterprise until two fundamental questions were answered: what was he doing on this earth, and what was the purpose of this life? Not knowing made life unbearable.

"This man, Oswell, had two good friends. One was a famous Harley Street specialist called Pagnam. The other was a small, round man, another specialist, whose name I cannot recall. They had the same qualities as Oswell. They knew someone in Paris, they said, who could cure me. I went to see this man in Paris."

He trailed off, becoming deeply thoughtful.

"And did he cure you?"

"He did, eventually."

He was lost in thought again.

"And did you—"

"It was a modest flat, near the Arc de Triomphe. He was old, had a great shaven head like a Tartar, and had a flowing white moustache. We had coffee in this tiny storeroom. It smelled like a Turkish or Greek shop—cheese, sausage, halva, spices. I was surprised that he spoke Russian so well. He told me that he could cure me but that it would cost a great deal of money. When he told me how much, I just laughed, thanked him for the coffee, got up, and left. It was a fantastic sum! I was already on the stairs when he called out to me. He said, 'The man you sent to the hospital prison in Kazan has already forgiven you.'

"I was astonished. I had never mentioned Päts in London. I found myself back in the storeroom, hardly knowing how I had got there.

"'Is he still alive?' I asked. He gazed at me calmly. My frantic thoughts ceased.

"'The guilt that you feel possesses you is not your fundamental problem.'

"'What is my problem?'

"'You do not accept your life.'

"'What is it that I do not accept?'

"'You believe that a great injustice was done to you as a child.'

"'I spent years in self-pity; how can I get rid of this terrible feeling of injustice?'

"'Justice, objective justice, is a big thing. It applies not only to individuals but also to families—back many generations—and to whole nations. Some members of one nation commit a grave sin. The whole nation must pay, must suffer, perhaps for 2,000 years.

"'Your grandfather does something against his conscience. He sows. Now he is dead, and you must reap. This is not injustice. You must not think of it egoistically. This responsibility is a great honour for you. If you accept it, you can repair the past of your father, your grandfather, and your great-grandfather. If you accept this, your being will grow.

"'Justice is not concerned with your little troubles. It is concerned with big things. It is ridiculous to think that God should be occupied with these little things, instead of you—'

"'But I cannot make this commitment now—'

"'You cannot do anything now. You are sick. You must rest much; even that you cannot do by yourself. I will help you.'

"The old man stood up, stepped back from the little table, and leaned back against the shelves."

Sirel sat slumped at the table. Although emotionally drained and physically exhausted himself, he thought he had never seen anyone so tired as the old man standing opposite him. For some reason, he could not take his eyes off him. Sirel began to feel an unexpected upsurge of energy. The old man was concentrating on him in a strangely intense, though impersonal way. Suddenly, it was as if a kind of blue-tinged, sheet lightning flashed out of the Russian and entered into him, and all his terrible weariness of months just fell away. At the same moment, the old man seemed to crumple, and his face turned a dirty grey, as if all life was draining out of him. Sirel could only stare, transfixed.

"You are all right now," the Russian murmured. "I must go."

He was back in about twenty minutes, and again, Sirel was astonished. The old man who had left the room was transformed. He was smiling broadly as if he could not hide his appetite for life.

"He cured you, but you didn't pay him?"

"He told me that if I wished to repay him, I could do so by taking part in an important experiment."

"What kind of experiment?"

Sirel gazed at me as if trying to decide something.

"The experiment involved the use of drugs."

I stared at him, waiting for him to go on.

"According to this old man—"

"Doesn't he have a name?"

"Let's just call him 'Ivanovitch.'"

"Okay."

"According to Ivanovitch, from the most ancient times, priestly castes on every continent have made use of certain alkaloids—sacred drinks—the inhalation of the smoke of certain substances. That there existed a very ancient tradition in the scientific application of these substances, with the aim of producing precise psychic states."

"What was the purpose?"

"To have a look ahead; to see, for a moment, that there is another reality and that, compared to that reality, ordinary reality is a dream."

"And after the experiment?"

"We conducted the same experiment time after time, with exactly the same result. I needed no persuasion from Ivanovitch. I became convinced of my own accord. Ivanovitch told me that, to achieve the same result without drugs and to make that result permanent, I would need to strive for the remainder of my life."

"Why would you do that?"

"Two reasons. First, by commencing this striving, I would begin to cure myself. Second, I would thereby pay for the cure by helping Ivanovitch confirm certain experiences which he had had in his early life."

"Such as?"

"According to Ivanovitch, fragments of the most ancient knowledge are locked up in various shrines, tombs, artefacts, and monuments in remote places all over the world, some of them in Ireland. And that the only way to access this knowledge is by the use of these ancient, sacred substances. He wished to establish, objectively, that this could be done by anyone who had been prepared in a certain way."

"Did you take part in experiments which prove that?"

"I'm not interested in proving anything. I'm relating my experiences to you."

"How is this connected to the experience I had in Austria?"

"Ivanovitch told me that he had cured a compatriot of mine before the War—a certain Baroness Schambok. This woman, he told me, had a rare psyche—that in very ancient times, such a woman would have been a temple priestess, what on the continent of Atlantis was called a pythoness."

I stared at him. He seemed perfectly serious. There was a wry or perhaps regretful smile on his face.

"I haven't heard the term 'pythoness' before."

"Again, according to this old man, before the demise of the continent of Atlantis, priests—who, he claims, were also at that time scientists—had anticipated some great cataclysm which was about to befall the planet earth. For that reason, these priest-scientists were scattered all over the planet, conducting experiments in an attempt to establish exactly what would happen. According to him, they communicated by telepathy through the medium of these pythonesses, who, in a deep trance, received and transmitted messages."

"Are you saying that Irma is something like that?"

"Ivanovitch told me that Irma could anticipate the moment and the manner of my death."

"Is that what I witnessed?"

"Not exactly. What you witnessed was an event which has taken place countless times."

"I don't understand that."

"You're familiar with the idea of eternal recurrence?"

"Yes."

"What you saw was an example of my death, recurring eternally. Ivanovitch told me that this time, it's possible for something different to happen."

"What could possibly change that situation?"

"Only a great sacrifice could change it."

"What kind of sacrifice?"

"The kind of sacrifice that constitutes a payment. Someone would have to lay down his life for me. Then I would not have to live this life again."

"Could Irma manipulate these visions?"

"Irma can only transmit exactly what she receives."

"Could I ask you something?"

"Of course you can."

"If you were unable to believe in the things people usually believe in—ambition, fame, success, the accumulation of wealth, and so on—how could you possibly function in life?"

"I had to *choose* to believe."

꧁꧂

There was a sudden subdued commotion as the Saudi got to his feet. Some of the Americans were voicing their regret that he had to leave so soon, but it seemed that he had an important meeting and that he was obliged, therefore, to leave them for the moment. He informed them that he hoped to be with them for dinner, and with that, he swept out. As he passed us, he nodded curtly to Sirel, who responded in like manner.

"There, I'm afraid, we'll have to leave it," said Sirel, consulting his watch. "Are you in town this evening?"

"I can be if we could meet up again."

"Meet me here, in the Horseshoe Bar, at eight o'clock. Is that okay?"

"Okay."

Inside the horseshoe-shaped counter, under the clock, the barman was a still-life study in discretion or indifference. Sirel and the Saudi were the only customers, perched on stools. The Saudi executed a dry little handshake, dismounted as he might from a camel, and walked past me with hardly a glance.

"So how did it go?" I asked.

Sirel was staring into the distance as if he could see a line of Bedouins crossing the sand dunes.

"Everything's arranged," he said dryly.

"What does that mean?"

"It means that, at the conclusion of protracted negotiations, a time and a place have been agreed for the exchange with Zdanov."

"Exchange of what exactly?"

"An ancient golden diadem will be exchanged for a death certificate, both items to be authenticated on site, following which, two fragile human beings will be exchanged, hopefully intact."

It was ironic, close to cynical.

"How is the diadem to be authenticated?"

"Zdanov has a healthy mistrust of experts. He wants Irma there to authenticate the diadem."

"Who'll authenticate the death certificate?"

"We'll have an expert there from the Swiss bank. If he's satisfied, that's all we need."

"How will the exchange of hostages be arranged?"

"That process," he said dryly, "is not so different."

"When and where does this all take place?"

"In Finland, one week from now."

"I have a question."

"Yes?"

"If Irma is going to be in Finland, doesn't that mean that the diadem, currently in your possession, is the real one?"

"That's correct!"

"So what about the fake you had made?"

Sirel considered me as if an offensive odour had been introduced into his presence.

"Let's call it a copy for the moment, shall we?"

"Okay. Who has it?"

Sirel's smooth irony could quickly elide into cold cynicism.

"When friend Bremer was intercepted, whilst intercepting the Greek's art thief, it was thought expedient to employ a certain sleight of hand where the diadem was concerned."

"You mean your friend in Geneva has the copy, thinking he has the original? Isn't that dangerous?"

Sirel was nodding, in an absent-minded sort of way.

"I would say that that's a pretty accurate assessment of the situation."

The barman had discreetly come to life and was passing a cloth with thoughtful deliberation across a perfectly clean section of counter.

"I don't understand this idea of sacrifice."

Sirel came back from very far away and gazed at me as if he had forgotten why I was there.

"I have a question for you," he said quietly. His intensity once again reminded me of Hilge.

"Yes?"

"In the vision you saw, of the death of the king with the golden mask, did you see the face of the woman or of the man who plunged the dagger into his neck?"

"No, the faces were . . . sort of blank."

"But you knew who they were?"

I felt a sudden, terrible tension in the region of my solar plexus. Instinctively, I knew that it was resistance to seeing something below my normal level of awareness. Then as if something had burst like a bubble, I heard myself say, "Yes, it was Irma and Tofer!"

He nodded grimly, gazing at me as if in satisfaction. Then he relented.

"Sacrifice is a payment. Objective justice proceeds according to objective laws. What is paid for will be received."

"You implied that someone had to sacrifice his life to change your fate. Who would do that?"

He was still and silent for quite some time, only the blotched sallowness betraying his intensity.

"A man with nothing to lose who owes me his life," he said quietly.

Chapter 8

⚬ᵐᵐᵐ⚬

Ⓗ ELSINKI IS SAID to be one of the safest cities in the world. Clearly, Sirel didn't think so. The three cars huddled close to the pavement on quiet, residential Lonnrothinkatu, engines running, the wipers quietly pushing away the persistent snowflakes. No one spoke. Above the trees, down at the end, an electric sign blinked on and off, telling us that it was minus twenty-seven degrees Celsius. Sirel was in the middle car. The silent movie of his conversation with Irma went on earnestly, framed by the rear window.

At last, Vladi appeared again behind the old-fashioned, wrought iron gate of number 45A. It creaked open, and he was scanning the street, the big man behind him miming, slightly out of sync. They looked like Russians, with their fur hats.

Sirel and Irma got out, and then Vladi and the other man were escorting them across the street, carefully negotiating the smooth ice and frozen snow. They disappeared into the building. Icicles hung in jagged stalactites from the eaves above the fifth floor, where Kaisa Jarvinen's apartment was. I could imagine them going up in the ancient, clanking lift. The grandeur was somewhat run down, but it was still a good address.

Vladi was coming out of the apartment as Toivo and I arrived. They went back out together, presumably to oversee surveillance. I was the last in. Kaisa paused in mid-sentence to smile at me. She was in her seventies, soignée, erect, with a presence immediately tangible. The honey-blonde hair had faded, but the grey-blue eyes had the same warm intensity of the sepia photo in Sirel's flat. We had got on so well together, visiting museums, looking at the great Finnish painters in the Ateneum, laughing together in the trams as they negotiated the city hills.

"We were talking about the Jewish Question," said Sirel.

I nodded. It was a coded message, telling me that things were going according to plan. I was not comfortable with the idea of manipulating a situation involving Kaisa. She had been largely instrumental in organizing the escape of some 3,000 Jews from Estonia in August 1941.

"Tell us about Marshal Mannerheim," I said on cue.

Kaisa smiled, looking pleased, and concentrated as if to remember:

It was 1940. In March that year, Mannerheim had been forced to surrender 16,000 square miles of Finnish territory to the Russians. By June, his British allies seemingly defeated at Dunkirk, Mannerheim felt obliged to seek an alliance with Hitler. Kaisa was appalled. She had gone to Mannerheim's spartan office at Mikkeli, demanding to know what would happen to Finland's 1,700 Jews.

The seventy-three-year-old aristocrat, commander-in-chief of the Finnish Defense Forces, sat calmly as always behind his desk, stroking his moustache, hearing her out.

"You know what one of our Jewish officers said to me, Kaisa? He said, 'The Winter War gave us Jews a deeper consciousness of being Finnish, and of belonging to Finland. More than any other period in our history.'"

"Sir, my information is, that since you made this alliance with Hitler, Wehrmacht and Waffen-SS officers are already in the country—"

"That's right. The SS-Panzergrenadierdivision 'Wiking' is already in training in Nummi-Pusula. And the man you are proposing to marry—Peeter Sirel—is at this moment in training with them."

She had blushed furiously then, and he had smiled, not unkindly. She was the best journalist he knew, and he had seen to it that she was decorated after the War.

"However," he continued, "there is one group that will never set foot in Finland—the Einsatzgruppen. So your Jews are safe."

As she told the story, the passion of past events gripped her, and she didn't seem to notice how Sirel and Irma sat like studies in concentration. Suddenly she paused and looked at us. Sirel glanced at me with a barely perceptible nod.

"Kaisa," I said, "what was the origin of this interest in the Jews?"

She came out of reverie, smiled at me then turned to Sirel.

"You remember the Romanische Café in Berlin, 1936?"

He nodded with a faint smile. It was where they had first met. It was a case of love at first sight. For her, the city was an elaborate stage set, electric with excitement. For him, the eleventh Olympic Games he was reporting on was a cynical Nazi exercise in international diplomacy. He had awakened her to what was happening to the Jews of Europe.

As Europe correspondent for a national newspaper, Kaisa had made it her mission in life to warn Jews everywhere of the terrible thing to come. But she had encountered an unexpected problem. The whole of Jewish Europe seemed as if mesmerized. When she interviewed them, urging them to get out while there was still time, they smiled, these sophisticated, wealthy Jews. They appreciated her concern, they told her suavely. They hinted that they had "plans." To her horror, she realized that they would do nothing until it was too late. There was something unstoppable in Kaisa's narrative flow.

"I woke up one night from a sweat-soaked nightmare. I was on a train which was hurtling along at top speed. The names of the stations were a blur as we swept past—Dachau, Buchenwald, Birkenau. We didn't stop—the platforms were packed with the staring ghosts of Jews who had already died. Nobody looked out the windows of the train, because there was a party in full swing, and the warnings I kept repeating went unheard. One man was drunk, playing patience at a table and I—"

She broke off abruptly, staring into space. She seemed to sink into her chair. I had the strangest impression that the vibrant, magnetic Kaisa I knew had suddenly departed her body, leaving an empty shell.

"Ask her what she's thinking about," I heard Sirel's voice saying.

It took me several moments to realize where his voice had sounded. I found myself staring at him. Sweat stood out in beads on my forehead. He was gazing at me, a slight smile on his face. It was as if he had not used words but that I had heard his voice in my chest, near the heart. I heard it again. This time it was definitely a voice in my chest, quite clear. He repeated his command.

"Ask her what she's thinking about now."

In a kind of daze, I heard my voice say quite clearly to Kaisa, "What are you thinking about now?"

"Sorry?" she started as if awakened from a daydream. "About nothing!" She smiled weakly, apologetic, but also clearly puzzled by the question.

"Go on!" said Sirel's voice in my chest.

"But what about the Jews? You said just now that it became the whole purpose of your life to warn them of the impending Holocaust. That so much suffering was of their own making, because the warning signs were clearly there. That German guilt would not be erased for generations and so on. Do you still think that?"

"I don't know really," she said uncertainly. "Did I say that?"

"Yes, you did. You said that the Germans could not wipe out their enormous crime against the Jews simply by pouring money into various projects, that their crime must be paid for, sooner or later, and that there were senior figures in German politics who felt no remorse, only resentment that the Nazis had been defeated."

Kaisa listened carefully to every word, studying me as if I were a complete stranger.

"Yes?" she said at length. "How odd!. I don't remember anything about it."

"But aren't you interested in these issues?"

"No, they don't interest me at all."

"But are you not concerned that such a thing could conceivably happen again; that the original attitudes are still in place; that—"

She shook her head as though with regret.

"I don't understand what you're talking about. I have no interest in this question, and I know nothing about it."

Her eyes were strangely blank, and her mouth hung open. There was something almost primitive about her.

"You said that you felt deeply that your family had betrayed its Jewish heritage. That when your famous Jewish ancestor managed to get into the faculty of medicine at Turku University back in the eighteenth century—by the simple device of converting to Christianity—it was a cynical exercise in survival. That your family had lived a lie for generations because of the wealth he bequeathed them. That it had been up to you to make reparations, to pay for their sins and omissions."

She gave no reply.

"Do you still think that?"

"I'm not thinking about it at all."

"If you were asked what you would like right now, what would you say?"

She glanced at me in wonder and then gazed slowly around the room as if looking for something.

"Think," I prompted. "What would you like?"

She fixed her gaze on the little table which separated us from Irma and Sirel. On it was the box of Belgian chocolates I had brought her. She made a tentative, pointing gesture towards the chocolates.

With a childlike twist of her head, she said, in a small voice, "I'd like some sweets."

There was something shocking about it, but it had charm too.

"Take two sweets and give them to her," said Sirel's voice. I jumped. It was like a vibration in my chest. I did as I was told.

She unwrapped the first one noisily and, with obvious relish, began to chew. There was no trace of self-consciousness.

"What have you done?" I demanded of Sirel.

To my astonishment, I realized that I had communicated in the same wordless way.

"I have taken away her personality. For the moment," his voice said in my chest.

"She will come to no harm. And she will remember nothing. We have not finished yet!" he added tersely.

Kaisa finished the second sweet and then gazed curiously at Irma and Sirel. Irma rose and beckoned wordlessly to Kaisa. Obediently, she rose and approached Irma shyly, as a child would. Irma raised her hands slowly to Kaisa's hair and gently, like a mother, began to remove the pins. Her hair fell in a crinkled mass halfway down her back, and she shook her head to help the process. Slowly, Irma raised the golden diadem and placed it on her head. It was another shock for me. I recognized in this older woman the Helen I had seen on the ship approaching Troy.

Irma guided her back to the couch and helped her to sit. Kaisa seemed dazed and began to look agitated. There was silence for several minutes as we watched her. Some strong emotion was working in her.

"Ask her what she's seeing now," said Sirel's voice in my chest.

"What are you seeing now?" I asked in a loud, clear voice. As instructed previously, I avoided using her name.

Her mouth began to work, her eyes screwed tightly shut. She began mumbling in some incomprehensible language. I realized, as if she too were speaking in my chest, that I could understand what she was saying.

"Menelaus is coming, there, there—through the dust!"

She pointed to some unseen distance, her eyes tightly shut. She paused. She was pointing again. Her body language indicated that she was seeing something down below as if from a height, perhaps from the top of the city walls.

"I see the bodies . . . of all those young men, the flies settling on their gaping wounds. Settling on their eyes . . . still open."

A terrible, primordial groan came out of her. It was a shocking sound which seemed to fill the room. I felt the hairs standing up on the back of my neck.

"They're dead because of me—the whore of Troy!"

This time, a kind of wailing rose from the depths of her being and gradually subsided into a dry, hopeless sobbing. I listened and watched her with a kind of horrified fascination.

"Who is Menelaus?" I heard my voice saying, strongly and clearly.

"My husband! Look at him! Look at him," she said urgently, again pointing to an unseen distance.

"Close your eyes!" said Sirel's voice peremptorily in my chest.

I closed my eyes. Suddenly, I felt myself gasping and choking. The hot, dry dust clogged my nostrils as a charging chariot came to an abrupt halt, the reined-in horses snorting and smelling strongly of acrid sweat. A huge, ugly man descended. Ferocious intent had fixed his features in a brutal mask. He halted his lumbering, wrestler's gait, staring fixedly through the dust at the warriors striding towards us. I sensed him focus on the swaggering young dandy who led them, a leopard-skin incongruously draped over his light armour. I knew immediately that this was Alexandros, or Paris, and that he was a worthless creature, with a kind of boyish, cheap charm. I was amazed that a woman of Helen's calibre could have fallen for such a man. Suddenly, he spotted Menelaus, and terror congealed on his features. He halted and seemed to shrink back into the ranks relentlessly advancing and carrying him forward as if to his doom.

Suddenly, it was as if I were inside the body of Menelaus, experiencing his feelings as my own. I felt the focus of his hatred. I saw me hacking Alexandros with systematic deliberation, throwing the pieces to left and right; saw scavengers' beaks rending the boyish face, claws tearing the handsome, insolent body. I experienced the sheer frustration of finding that the disgusting little coward had disappeared as if into thin air.

Then I was up on the ramparts. My head moved inside Helen's head as she glanced at the top of the wall behind. Her feelings were of utter despair, her thoughts suicidal. I felt the wall suddenly slip away and the brown earth rushing up to meet me; my whole life flashing past, with details that—

"Leave it!" said Sirel's voice peremptorily in my chest.

I got such a shock that I opened my eyes. It was exactly like surfacing from a deep sleep. For several moments, the room before me made no sense. I realized that I had to focus in a particular way as if to reconstruct what we refer to as "reality." The impression that what I was seeing was simply a construct was very strong. Gradually, as if through force of habit, I found myself accepting it once again as "reality."

At the end of the long couch we both sat on, Kaisa appeared to have fallen into a deep sleep. Irma and Sirel sat still as before, gazing calmly at me.

"Don't move!" Sirel commanded in his normal voice. I stayed still.

"We need to complete the experiment," he said, looking severe. I nodded.

It was as if we had a tacit agreement that I would follow instructions, on the understanding that my curiosity was stronger than fear or reservation.

"Close your eyes!"

I closed them.

Blackness became a night sky. Two mountain peaks emerged, dark silhouettes, faint stars behind. I realized that I could see clearly in the dark. A cluster of buildings stood on an outcrop of rock, guarding the pass between the two mountains. A sound emanated faintly from there, like the distant swarming of bees. As soon as I concentrated on the sound, I was whisked at tremendous speed across a valley towards it, and then I was inside a great hall. Below me, servants held torches aloft, forming a great rectangle. Inside it, ranks of warriors stepped out a slow march, in time to a requiem, which rose and fell in great waves of sound like surf on some desolate shore. The voices of the women, lining the walls in the shadows, rose in a high, keening wail. The bass voices of the men seemed to answer in counterpoint, the funereal rhythm punctuated by the slap of leather, in unison, on the stone floor.

With each step, the warriors executed a complicated series of movements. There were six sets of these, involving seemingly unrelated positions for head, arms, and legs. I was immediately reminded of the beauty and precision of Irma's temple dance. These, however, were ritualized fighting positions, each one accompanied by a group of words from a chant, each series ending with the name "Ag-am-em-non"!

In the centre of the room was a great stone plinth on which reposed the body of the dead king whose murder I had witnessed. On his face was the golden mask, reflecting the flickering light. The warriors marched in an unbroken circle, round and round the plinth. Suddenly, with a great slap of leather on stone, everything halted in unison. Men and women stood completely still and silent. A faint, rustling sound began, and six men, who looked like members of a priestly caste, emerged from the shadows. They formed a hexagon around the plinth. As soon as they did, I realized that I was in the same room where I had witnessed the murder of the king. At the same time, I saw again a scene which in horror I had completely suppressed. After the murder, when everyone else had fled in fear, these six priests had entered and spoken earnestly to the dying king. One had drawn the knife slowly from the king's neck. Another filled a goblet with his gushing blood. A filmy something rose from the body and disappeared. He was dead. The six priests solemnly drank in turn from the goblet. I was so agitated, I knew I was going to open my eyes—

"Calm down!" commanded Sirel's voice in my chest. Instantly, I was calm.

I was witness again to the silent ranks of warriors and the priests forming a hexagon around the plinth. Everyone was still. I heard the distant humming sound again. A replica of the corpse, a misty ghost, hovered vertically above the king's body. It seemed to tremble or vibrate with a light so intense that it was impossible to look at it directly. I looked at the priests. They all had their eyes closed, heads bowed in deep concentration. I had the distinct impression that they were somehow in communication with the image hovering above. The light radiated to all six points, like tongues of flame, deflecting inwards through the priests' bodies, connecting all points of the hexagon in a living symbol. I had no doubt that I was witnessing something both sacred and magical. The humming sound increased and deepened as if coming from the throats of all the men.

"Open your eyes!" commanded Sirel's voice.

He was staring at me as if assessing my state. I felt as if all the blood had drained from my face, as if life itself was being pulled down through my fundament into the earth. I had a desperate need to get back to what we normally refer to as "reality," to reassure myself that it existed.

"You need to rest!" said Sirel forcefully. "Start talking. Ask me anything you like!"

At that moment, Kaisa stirred and groaned. Irma rose and went to her. She removed the diadem, difficult because her head had fallen forward. Then gently, with the greatest care, she began putting up Kaisa's hair again. Kaisa protested, still asleep, pushing away her hands as a child would.

The whole story, starting with Aleks Kallas, seemed to pass before my eyes.

"Tell me the real meaning of Aleks Kallas's part in this story," I said.

According to Aleks Kallas's manuscript, he and his partisans liberated Tallinn on 16 August 1941 in just short of seventeen hours, ahead of the advance German forces. According to official German war records, Tallinn was liberated by German forces on 27 July.

There is considerable evidence that Kallas's version is true and that the Germans suppressed the story, rewriting this particular piece of history.

The Kallas version ends with a curious incident: as German Stukas roared overhead, bombing escaping Russian ships in the harbour, the partisans stumbled on a group of about 4,000 demoralized people, abandoned on the docks by the escaping Russian commissars. Some 3,000 of these were Jews, promised escape to Russia for their part in the defence of Tallinn against the Germans. The remaining 1,000 were stragglers from various Red Army units. These latter voluntarily laid down their arms. They were in a shocking state, many without boots, their wounds roughly dressed in blood-soaked bandages. Sirel and Kersting had immediately taken charge of the Jews, who were escorted south to Kalda Farm, Kallas's childhood home, and hidden in the swamps. Later, with the aid of Finnish journalist Kaisa Jarvinen and her contacts in the intelligence section of the Finnish RVL Border Guard Unit—and certainly with the knowledge of Marshal Mannerheim—they were spirited by Sirel in September 1941 through southern Finland to Lapland. From thence, they were taken to Sweden and then onward to the United States.

According to what Sirel told me then in Kaisa's apartment, Kallas had been promised a substantial share of gold bullion—yet to be stolen—in return for his help, as had Kersting. In the end, Kallas resented these moves, because they took the real leadership away from him and appealed to something less admirable in him. He also resented the fact that Sirel knew he wanted the money and had read him well.

"Aleks suffered from self-pity," said Sirel. "When the War was over and he found himself in Sweden, he didn't know what to do with his life. It was as if there was nothing more to live for. He blamed me for everything. Self-pity is a disease of the emotions. I should know—I suffered from it all my life until I met Ivanovitch in Paris after the War. Aleks could have started a new life. Instead, he chose to fritter away his talents, his whole life, in a quiet backwater in Ireland. This is typical of the way in which self-pity works. It says,

'Why should I do anything when life has played such a dirty trick on me?' It's exactly how a depressed man thinks. Aleks suffered from bouts of deep depression. Did you know that?"

"No, I didn't. Was Hans Kersting the same?"

"Now you've put your finger on it. He was exactly the same."

He looked at Irma. She nodded as if in confirmation. Kaisa had gone back into a deep sleep, her head propped back more comfortably by Irma. Sirel was right. Talking had restored my confidence in the existence of "reality." There was something different about him. It was as if some primordial tension in him had relaxed. It seemed to change the contours of his face. I knew it had to do with seeing a different version of his death. He was gazing at me, smiling faintly, as if reading my thoughts.

"The death we witnessed," he said quietly, "means that I do not have to live this life again."

"You could have seen this yourself. Why did you need me?"

His eyes had suddenly gone cold. He said severely, "There must be a witness. That is the rule. This was a great privilege for you!"

Irma was nodding.

He glanced at her and then said to me, "We have not finished. There is one more thing that must be seen. But you are free to leave now, if you wish."

We gazed at each other a long moment. We both knew I wasn't leaving.

"Close your eyes," he commanded quietly.

Blackness gave way to grey dawn. I was approaching the mouth of a cave, halfway up the mountain. A strong odour assailed my nostrils, reminding me instantly of an animal's cage. A woman with long, greasy, greying hair sat on the floor inside. Flames from sconces lit burnished gold ornaments, life-size, of venomous snakes, which were draped about her neck and shoulders, their fierce heads poised in attacking position. She sat above a deep fissure in the floor, from which rose a strongly sulphuric vapour, sickly sweet. She was in a deep trance. It was Irma. I heard the distant humming sound again but could not determine its source. She suddenly became agitated, and her whole body began to tremble violently. She mouthed incomprehensible sounds like someone in the grip of a nightmare. The humming sound increased in volume, and I felt myself spinning as if through a tunnel.

Suddenly, I was in a place of deathly quiet, a white world with a deep carpet of virgin snow. Pockets of snow rested precariously on branches of trees, undisturbed by any wind. I felt like a camera pointed in one direction with no human will to focus me. I was in a forest clearing. To the left, propped against a large granite boulder, was the Irma I knew. She was in a sitting position, quite still, her eyes closed. Her right arm hung limp, her hand clutching the golden diadem, which lay on the snow alongside. I knew with certainty that she was dead. Her face was grey in repose, the flat rock behind her head smudged red with blood. Strange sounds intruded, like giant hornets roaring towards us, but were snatched away by the wind at the last moment, before fading as quickly into oblivion with a hissing noise. The distant humming sound increased in volume until I thought I couldn't stand it.

"Open your eyes!" said Sirel's voice in my chest.

I experienced the same shock and subsequent disorientation. By the time I had reaffirmed reality, I found myself gazing at the Irma I had just seen in the forest clearing. She was seated beside Sirel as before, her face a dirty white, her eyes open and staring at me. On her lap, her right hand clutching it, was the golden diadem.

"What you have witnessed," she said, her speech strangely slurred, "is my death."

She spoke as if her lips were already becoming stiff in death. She looked dreadful. Slowly, she looked down and gazed for quite some time at the diadem.

Kaisa came to with a start. She looked around, somewhat sheepishly.

"Gosh, sorry, I must have—"

"Don't worry, Kaisa," I immediately interjected, with a reassuring smile. "You must have been really tired. It was all that shopping and running around yesterday!"

I had been well primed by Sirel. He had anticipated every eventuality.

"What did I miss?" she asked, obviously recovering quickly.

"Oh, getting the Jews out of Estonia in 1941. I wanted to ask you, Kaisa, is that what took you to Estonia at that time?"

Kaisa drew a deep breath, sat up straight, and patted her hair. She was clearly her old self again.

"Well," she said, with a little smile, "I got my paper to send me there to cover the German liberation of Tallinn. The real reason was to see my handsome young husband—taken from me once again by the War."

She gazed rather sadly at him. He returned the look as if he had caught the mood. There were 4,381 Jews in Estonia just before the War. The disappearance and subsequent escape of 3,000 of them was followed by a nationwide hunt to root out the remaining 1,381. By 15 December 1941, thanks largely to the activities of SS division commander Alfons Rebane, every last one of them had been murdered, mostly in Belzec concentration camp, where Tofer and Poom were then stationed.

In June 1941, as Sirel was being parachuted into Estonia, 500 Jewish refugees were arriving in Finland. Kaisa had thrown herself wholeheartedly into the task of getting 350 of them out to Sweden. Meanwhile, the remaining 150 were stranded in Finland. All the time, the Gestapo was in contact with sympathizers in the Finnish State Police to try to get them deported to German-held territory.

One year later, in June 1942, as she sped towards Imatra to cover the visit of Hitler, Kaisa could think of nothing but her Jewish refugees. Ironically, they were trapped on the island of Suursaari, like chickens behind wire, while she was on her way to interview the fox.

A month after Hitler's visit, Finnish State Police moved the Jews from Suursaari to Helsinki and arrested ten others, but Mannerheim and President Risto Ryti had moved quickly to prevent deportation. On 6 October, however, the state police moved very quickly and managed to deport twenty-eight persons, nine of them Jews, to Nazi-occupied Estonia. Kaisa immediately got herself sent to Tallinn. It was too late to do anything. The Gestapo had already transported them to Birkenau. She spent the evening of her arrival in the Du Nord Club, talking to Sirel. She was deeply saddened by the almost certain death of the nine Jews. Sirel had different preoccupations. It was the last time they were to meet until long after the War was over. By then, it was too late for both of them. I didn't know what Kaisa meant by that, and it didn't seem the right moment to ask. We all lapsed into a rather sad, thoughtful silence.

There was a discreet knock on the door of the flat. Sirel glanced at his watch.

"Come in!" he called.

Vladi walked in slowly and stood holding the door. He was looking at Irma.

"It's time to go," he told her.

She gazed blankly at him for a long moment. Then she rose, slowly and solemnly placed the diadem in a kind of hatbox, and walked wordlessly with it towards the door. There she turned and spoke directly to Sirel.

"Where do you propose to keep me?"

This was the old imperious, demanding Irma. Sirel was just as formal and distant in manner.

"You will be kept in a safe place, quite comfortably, until the meeting tomorrow. You will keep the diadem with you, at all times, as agreed. Do you have any questions?"

"No questions!"

With that, she swept out, Vladi following.

❦

Chapter 9

⟨ɷɷɷ⟩

FROM HELSINKI, WE drive to an isolated farm at the end of a long inlet on the south-west coast. There's a battered wooden house there, called Sommervik, which seems to sit out among the tall reeds. A long jetty runs out to a cluster of rocks, on which a boathouse perches precariously. In winter, it's the bleakest place I know, and that's when I first saw it. I didn't know at the time that it belonged to Sirel, and I wouldn't have cared if I had known. Overnight, the temperature had dropped from a mere minus twenty-seven degrees Celsius to minus thirty-two. The wind chill factor lowered the temperature another ten degrees.

There is only one long, winding road down to the farm. Our tracks had been obliterated overnight, and the only way to know where the deep drains were on either side was by the tall marker poles which stuck up out of the snow banks.

We were in the little summer house back up in the trees, overlooking the farm buildings below and facing the road. Sirel stood rock-still at the window, staring down through binoculars.

"They're here," he murmured.

Soon, we could make out the three cars slowly snaking up the road through the trees. The snipers could have picked them off anytime, but that wasn't going to happen. They turned cautiously into the yard below, with a soft, crunching sound, and pulled right up to the circular stone wall of the well. It was a silent movie in slow motion. No one moved, and there was an eerie silence, the wind moaning mournfully in the treetops. One car door opened and then another. Then they were standing by the cars, really looking like Russians now—even Tofer—all with fur hats, gloves, and mufflers. Zdanov moved with arrogant assurance among the watchful heavies, striding without hesitation up onto the veranda and in through the squat farmhouse door. Habermel got out slowly and awkwardly. He was a big man, but he looked pale under his tan. He was handcuffed and manacled. From behind, one of the heavies plonked a fur hat on his white hair and pushed him forward with arrogant indifference. I saw Sirel's knuckles whiten on the binoculars.

For some time, absolutely nothing seemed to happen. Sirel had not moved from his position at the window, binoculars trained downwards. No one spoke. Then Vladi went into a fit of slow, horrible coughing. Sirel turned round once to look at him, exchanged looks with Toivo, and then went back to his watching.

"Look!" I said quietly, and pointed.

Sirel's binoculars moved slowly upward. Smoke was curling up lazily from the chimney of Sommervik.

Suddenly, Sirel's walkie-talkie started crackling. He grabbed it, listened intently, and then rattled off some cryptic reply in Russian. I saw the door of Sommervik open. Men with high-powered rifles walked out and disappeared in different directions into the trees, behind and above the house. Sirel turned and nodded to Vladi. It marked the beginning of a strange, ritualized game. The stakes were high, and it was played out like slow-motion chess, because there was no margin for error.

Toivo had wordlessly taken over from Sirel. From where I stood, I could see Sirel helping Vladi put his overcoat on, just inside the bedroom door. It seemed to take a long time. Vladi moved like an old man, looking quite ill. Then they were standing in the kitchen again. Slowly, Vladi turned and, to my surprise, embraced Sirel. He looked a long moment at Toivo then they too embraced. Wordlessly, Vladi opened the door into a whistling wind, and we watched him walk, ever so slowly, down the slope through the snow. He held a walkie-talkie in his gloved right hand.

There is a large, red-painted barn, converted for domestic use, halfway between Sommervik and the summer house we occupied. That was where the negotiations, verifications, and exchanges took place. As soon as Vladi arrived there, he was joined by his counterpart from Sommervik, a frowning lawyer with spectacles and briefcase. A few minutes later, two more men came down from the farmhouse. I learned later that they were officials from the Hermitage museum in St Petersburg. With that, the strange ritual continued. All the while, Sirel was at the window, speaking cryptically into the walkie-talkie.

First, Irma, elegant in a long fur coat and hat, was escorted down past our window. She picked her way carefully, clutching the hatbox, and Toivo was obliged to match her pace. The barn door closed behind them with a dull thud. They were in there for a long time. Then we saw Irma and the two Hermitage men, unhurriedly ascending the hill to Sommervik, and the two officials from the Swiss bank casually ascended the hill towards us. They presented Sirel with a certificate, verifying the death of Sasha Veinberg. Apparently, all was in order. There was a long silence then, with no movement from either side.

The walkie-talkie started crackling again. This time, the door of Sommervik was thrown open, and we saw Habermel standing there, his open coat blowing in the wind. The manacles were gone, but he was still handcuffed, the fur hat at a rakish angle on his head. One of the heavies was holding him by the left arm, waiting for something.

Oleksandr Yelahin had brought Bremer out from the back bedroom. Bremer was a surprise. He was slim, dark, and good-looking, in his early thirties. He had been allowed to shave and spruce himself up. Even with handcuffs on and Yelahin gripping him by the arm, he retained his air of arrogance and contained violence.

We watched and waited while the walkie-talkies crackled, and Sirel replied cryptically. They were synchronising the walk down of the two hostages.

Halfway down the slope, Bremer insisted on halting to see where Habermel was. We saw Yelahin speaking angrily and Bremer replying with that awful arrogance. Yelahin attempted to push him on, and Bremer fell to his knees like a footballer faking a foul. It was a tremendously tense moment. Habermel's escort had halted too and was speaking tensely into his walkie-talkie as was Yelahin into his. Beside the window, Sirel was issuing rapid, terse instructions in Russian. Somehow, the moment passed, and the two hostages were in the barn.

By mid-afternoon, it was all over, and the Russians had departed. Irma had left in the lead car with Tofer, Vladi in the second car with Zdanov. Within minutes of their departure, Toivo was following them. Zdanov's lawyer stayed as our hostage.

We stayed on in the little summer house. Sirel had gone into a catatonic stillness by the window, distant and uncommunicative. Oleksandr had been padding about restlessly, equally uncommunicative. I was leafing quietly through a magazine, knowing they were waiting for something, when the Russian lawyer started complaining again. In one swift movement, Olek was beside him, had grabbed him by the back of the hair, and shoved him down into a chair, snarling something slowly and carefully in Russian. The lawyer blanched, his eyes almost popping out of his head. He was as surprised as I was. Olek produced handcuffs, snapped one end over the lawyers left wrist and secured the other to a pipe near the stove. That's when I knew it wasn't over yet.

Dusk was closing in, and Olek had just switched on a lamp when a long, terrible groan came out of Sirel. It made my hair stand on end. Olek was immediately beside him, asking him something urgently in Russian. He replied briefly as if in anguish. He was still sitting by the window, deathly white, still as a corpse. I thought he was having a heart attack.

Oleksandr took me firmly by the sleeve and ushered me out.

"What's the matter?" I asked.

"Vladi's dead."

"How does he know?"

"Get your things. We're leaving."

On the way back to Helsinki, we were flagged down by the Liikkuva Poliisi, the Highway Police. There were three patrol cars parked right across the highway, their flashing lights swirling across the trees and snow, lurid in the darkness. The whole area had been cordoned off to preserve the scene, with traffic backed up on both sides. A white police bike came roaring up from behind and halted right beside us. A leather-suited policeman in high boots dismounted, pulling off his white helmet and one gauntlet, as if too hot. Sirel immediately called out something to him. The reply was cryptic. We could soon see why. Another patrolman arrived, and between them, they set about opening a filter lane to ease the backed-up traffic.

The car door nearest me suddenly opened, and to my surprise, Toivo slipped in. I slid across the seat to make room, and he put a heavy carpet bag between us. It made a clinking, metallic sound, like an old-fashioned tool bag. I took one look at his face and decided to hold any questions. Sirel didn't even look around. He murmured some question quietly in Estonian. Toivo just as quietly murmured a reply.

We were moving forward more quickly now. Then the policeman was waving us past in businesslike fashion. Inside the preserved area, a crater spanned one lane, and there were bits of metal and glass everywhere. The blast had torn off branches and blackened several tree trunks. One car had slammed into a tree, its nose all buckled. Footprints and dark smudges led away from it into the forest. I found myself staring at Toivo. His eyes were fixed on the car, his face like grey putty in the lurid light. We drove on for a good half hour in silence.

"That crater back there—"

"Zdanov's car; blown to bits. There's not much of anything left."

I stared at him in horror.

"But Vladi was in that car!"

He nodded, staring out the window.

"Yeah!" was all he said.

We sped along in silence again for some time.

"The car that crashed into the tree—"

Sirel had cut across me gruffly with another question, in Estonian—something about Irma. Toivo met Sirel's gaze briefly in the mirror and then looked at me.

"Irma got out of that car with horrific injuries and walked about twenty metres into the forest."

I stared at him in incomprehension.

"She's dead," he pronounced.

"About the crashed car—"

"Tofer was driver. He was killed outright."

It was like that the whole way to Helsinki. Answers to my questions tended to be monosyllabic. Basically, what had transpired was as follows: Vladi was dying of cancer and in considerable pain. He owed some debt to Sirel he could never repay. Zdanov posed a real threat to Sirel and to everyone connected to him. Zdanov had ruthlessly wiped out Vladi's immediate family, and Tofer his father and his brother's family. He considered it a privilege to be taken as hostage to guarantee safe conduct to Zdanov and his entourage. It gave him the opportunity to kill several birds with one stone, as it were. With this in mind, Vladi had been wired with high explosive. How it was wired and detonated, how it went undetected by KGB veterans, I could only guess. There was no point in asking. All I knew was that when Oleksandr Yelahin was in the KGB, he had been an explosives expert attached to some special ops unit. Maybe that was the real reason why he had been called in. Sirel said a curious thing, tacked on to the tail end of one of his monosyllabic utterances. He said that he had agreed to what Vladi wanted to do only when he had extracted from him a promise not to kill Zdanov and Tofer from motives of revenge. That if his sacrifice was to be worthwhile, it had to be made from very different motives. There was no point in asking Sirel to elaborate.

I could see the distant lights of Helsinki under a canopy of low cloud.

"Can I make an educated guess?" I asked Sirel.

"Concerning what?"

"This bag," I said, touching it. "It's the diadem, isn't it?"

He nodded ponderously, glancing at me in the mirror. I wondered why he drove himself.

"Close your eyes!" he suddenly commanded.

It took a moment to realize that his voice had sounded in my chest. I closed them. Immediately, a sound like giant hornets roared towards me but was snatched away by the wind at the last moment, before fading into oblivion with a hissing noise. I was in that place of deathly quiet again, that white world with a deep carpet of virgin snow. It was the same forest clearing. Irma was still there, propped against the large granite boulder. She was in the same sitting position, quite still, her eyes closed. Her right arm still hung limp, her hand clutching the golden diadem, which lay on the snow alongside. As before, I knew that she was dead. As before, I felt like a camera pointed in one direction with no human will to focus me. It registered the figure entering from the left as Toivo and the expression on his face as somewhere between wonder and pity. Gently, he removed the diadem from her grasp and placed her hand with the other one in her lap. He turned and walked away. She looked dignified, as if merely waiting for death to come. The roaring sound increased in volume, coming at me, dying suddenly with a fading, hissing sound. I realized it was the traffic out on the highway.

Row upon row of massive granite steps rise skyward to support the gigantic classical pillars fronting the parliament house. The man carefully negotiating his way down the steps in the bleak sunshine would have stood out anywhere in Helsinki. He was clearly a Russian of the wealthy, sophisticated type. He was tall, handsome, with a military bearing. I already knew that he was a senior diplomat. As he got near the bottom of the steps, he waved cheerfully to Sirel. I got an impression of a hearty, offhand personality who cared not a whit that he would be seen being picked up by an unofficial car. In a city full of watchful eyes, it showed the startling confidence of a true insider.

The negotiations took place in the Ateneum Art Museum. It had been the Russian's idea apparently. Toivo had gone off somewhere to park the car. Oleksandr and I had followed at a discreet distance while Sirel and the Russian walked slowly along, gazing briefly at the paintings like tourists, and talking in low, urgent tones. They had paused in front of Gallen-Kallela's *Väinämöinen's Voyage*. In the prow of the ship, the white-haired, bearded ancient gazed with sorrow or indifference at the naked maidens happily fixing flowers in their hair. The Russian gazed at them thoughtfully too whilst continuing his fluent exchange with Sirel. Suddenly, he turned to Sirel, fixed him with a serious look, and then with theatrical deliberation, extended his hand. There was a momentary hesitation on Sirel's part, and then his hand was being extended too. The body language told the whole story. We saw Toivo coming in through a door down at the end. He was surprised when we told him that the deal had already been struck. It meant that Sirel would receive the "recovery fee" he had wanted, in return for the golden diadem found at Troy.

The next stage was almost a formality, but it went on for a long time, in slow motion it seemed to me. Toivo and Oleksandr were both involved, making them intense and wary. They went to and fro, making phone calls. It had to do with providing certain guarantees to the Russian diplomat, checking and double-checking the transfer of an interim payment to a numbered account in Switzerland, in favour of Sirel.

By late afternoon, our business was finished. Lights were coming on as we sped through the city, heading back to Sommervik. Sirel was obliged to be in Finland for several weeks. I was invited to stay. I stayed for two weeks.

During the following weekend, Sirel received confirmation that everything had gone through, sooner than expected. Hilge had arrived, apparently to look after Habermel, who seemed none the worse for his ordeal. She had brought Sirel's granddaughter with her, and they had collected Kaisa en route. There was a general air of contained jubilation. There was to be a celebratory dinner on the Saturday evening. The ancient smoke sauna had been lit early. It was the women's turn first, as they had dinner to prepare. Later, when it was the men's turn, the mood was almost boisterous. I had never seen Sirel in such good spirits. Toivo and Olek went in and out, gasping for air because Sirel liked it so hot. I did too, but it was suffocating in there. I went out once or twice. Toivo and Olek rolled in the snow, clowning like schoolboys. I was full of questions, and I was hoping to speak to Sirel alone before I left. Finally, even Habermel left, and we could hear them showering and laughing over in the washroom. Sirel didn't seem to mind that I stayed. He threw more water on the stones, and the intense heat rendered us speechless. It was very silent and peaceful in there. A candle guttered inside the ancient lamp on the floor, throwing shadows on the dim and blackened timbers. Suspended above, we watched the candle, primeval, sweating ghosts from the dawn of Finland's history.

"Can I ask you something?"

"Sure!"

"Why was it so important for you to die a different death?"

"Do you know why you're on this earth?"

"Sorry?"

"You heard me."

He gazed at me with that ironic expression.

Slowly I said, "Back in Dublin, you said that it means you do not have to live this life again."

"But you don't know what that means either? Do you like legends or folk tales?"

"Yes."

"Name a favourite one. Maybe one you liked as a child."

I was puzzled. I knew he was insisting on suggesting a certain line of thought.

"*The Arabian Nights*; my favourite was the story of Aladdin." Sirel nodded.

"Close your eyes," he commanded. I closed them.

At first, I experienced only a spinning sensation and then a feeling of great calm and stillness. Something was warm under my bare feet. It was sand. And it was night, with warm winds. Over my head, an enormous navy sky was punctuated by brilliant stars which seemed liquid with life. There was a group of dark shadows across the desert, forming some kind of pattern, and a little tinkling sound came from there, like a bell shaken intermittently by the wind. I turned my right ear towards it as if cupping it to catch the sound, and instantly, I was pulled with tremendous force and speed towards it. Then I was inside a large tent, lit softly by an unseen lamp, the atmosphere heavy with sweet incense. Beautiful rugs covered the floor and walls, subtle silks billowed down like clouds. A little, old, wizened man sat upright on the floor, smoking some kind of long-stemmed pipe, surrounded by various brass utensils. He was gazing calmly at me. He was distinctly oriental, Mongolian or Chinese, with very long, thin moustaches. The astonishing thing was that something was in constant movement behind the calm, mask-like face as if all the faces that had been important in my life were flitting behind it. One of the more persistent faces was that of Sirel.

Suddenly, Sirel's voice was speaking in my chest, "Ask him anything you like!"

The old man was gazing at me expectantly. I wanted to speak, but words would not come. I wanted to ask him to explain the real story of Aladdin as if I were a child. As soon as I knew what I wanted, it was somehow communicated wordlessly to him. He was nodding. He told me this story, and I heard it in my chest, near the heart, as if Sirel were speaking, but it was like a dream.

"I am Al-lud-dinn. The story of the magic lamp, the genie, the Black Magician: all of that is my story. Now I want to tell a different story, a story just for you. When I was a child, my mother worried about me, because I was different. She knew that children's games embarrassed me. She knew, because I had told her so. Yes, children's games embarrassed me, because I remembered myself as an adult from some previous life. That part I didn't tell her! It made me very uncomfortable to be back again, living this same life, trapped in the body of a child. I was like an outsider, looking in through a window, at games which made no sense to me.

"I had a friend, Lin Po, who from his earliest years knew that he wanted to be a very rich merchant. And indeed, he became a very rich merchant. It struck me that he too had lived a previous life, only he didn't remember it! He remembered only each step which led him to riches.

"I had another friend, Sun Yen, who dreamed of becoming captain of the emperor's famous bodyguard. People said he would go very far. He went very far indeed, much too far. He achieved great power over other people but none over himself. He was the cause of great suffering, and many, many deaths.

"They were very interesting, these friends of mine. But when I was with them, I had to disguise myself, to howl like a wolf, as it were, so that I could run with these wolves. But their aims in life made no sense to me. I felt like someone on a strange and unfamiliar road, being carried along by a noisy multitude which was rushing headlong forward. I knew that on this road, I, at least, was going nowhere. I could see another, parallel road, one which would take me to my destiny. I knew that I needed help to get to this road and that I would get that help. I also knew that I must wait patiently and choose the moment with great care. I knew this in every detail, because it had all happened before in my previous existence. And I was still only a child!

"My father was dead. I should have been helping my poor mother. Instead, I roamed the city, with this vagabond gang of ragged street urchins. We were hungry as wolves, cunning as foxes! And she was happy, my mother, because I had turned out to be a normal boy. This was one game I did not mind playing, because I was in disguise, waiting for my destiny. That destiny began to unfold the day the Black Magician knocked on the door of our house. My mother thought he was just another street vendor, selling things from house to house. But I recognized him immediately! Of course, I pretended I had no idea who he was. But he knew who I was! He had been witness to that terrible moment in my previous life when I took a wrong turning; when I missed the turning which would have led to my destiny. My loss, on that occasion, was the Black Magician's gain. That moment was so painful that I remembered the pain in my new life as a child. I knew that this was my last chance, that the opportunity would never come again.

"This magician needed me as much as I needed him, because our destinies were intertwined. It was this which made it such a dangerous enterprise.

"The magician did lead me to my destiny. It gave a tremendous focus to my life. I never experienced again the pain and despair of meaninglessness. So long as I remembered myself, who I really was, and what my destiny was, I made no serious mistakes.

"Well, you know the story; the lamp, the genie, the riches, the gorgeous palaces—not forgetting the beautiful princess, my wife, who had travelled down a different road in my previous life. You know that in the end I triumphed. That means that I do not have to live this life again. It is finished."

"Open your eyes!" said Sirel's voice in my chest.

This time, the shock of returning to a different reality was even greater than before. I was amazed to find myself sitting in a sauna. My surroundings seemed alien, Aladdin's tent so much more real. I could not understand why tears were streaming down my face. I had been touched at an emotional level above or below my normal experience—I could not tell which. Sirel was gazing at me, looking concerned.

"I still don't understand," I said. My voice seemed to come from the depths.

"Your emotions have understood. Only at a certain emotional level can magic and legends be understood. Normally, you have no access to that level of emotion."

I stared at him in incomprehension.

"It's clear to me now that you have strange powers. How did you acquire them?"

Sirel threw his head back and laughed, taking me by surprise. Instantly, I felt something in me begin to relax. When he had recovered, he gazed at me for a long moment as if he was really fond of me.

"You think you can freely ask questions like that? Just like putting a coin in a machine so that a chocolate bar will pop out?"

"Why shouldn't I?"

He laughed briefly again as if in disbelief and shook his head at me.

"These things have to be paid for—in advance. People must pay and must be able to pay. And if people pay as much as this would cost, they would not talk. First, one must pay."

"You mean with money?"

He shook his head in theatrical fashion, still apparently amused by my questions.

"Not with money. No amount of money could buy what we are talking about."

"Are you talking about magic?"

"Magic has existed from the most ancient times and has never been lost. Magic and miracles are the same. For example, telepathy is a miracle. A miracle is the manifestation in this world of the laws of another world. And there are forty-eight orders of laws. People who know how to use and control the laws of nature are magicians."

I stared at him. The authority with which he had spoken intrigued me.

"How could you know such things?"

But he went on talking, more to himself than to me.

"Back in the dawn of history," he said softly, "before they became spoilt, people could communicate with each other—and even see what was going on—a great distance away."

He had gone completely still, in deep thought.

"How do you know that?"

He came back from very far away and blinked at me.

"It's simple. Such people still exist."

"Where do they . . . ?"

Instead of answering, he told me the following story.

In September 1941, Sirel was taking a large group of Jewish refugees from Estonia, across southern Lapland, en route to Sweden. Towards nightfall, they stumbled on a settlement of Lapps, who were astonished and alarmed to see several thousand unkempt, desperate-looking people advancing towards them. A gun went off, wounding Sirel in the head. He collapsed and was in a coma for several months. He regained consciousness one night to find himself inside a large, tent-like structure. The first thing he became aware of was that he was no longer in his body. He was somewhere above it, looking down, knowing he was already dead and that he was ready to depart. A very ancient Lapp elder, a kind of shaman as it turned out, stood at his feet below, looking up. Sirel became instantly aware that the shaman was calling to him without words and that this call was pulling him back down into his body. He re-entered his body and in a matter of days began to recover. He discovered that he had been taken to northern Lapland. Outside, the temperature hovered around minus fifty degrees Celsius, but he was perfectly comfortable and well inside. He stayed with the shaman and a small group of Lapps throughout the winter of 1941 and the spring of 1942. From the shaman he learned the use of magnetism and hypnotism for healing, as well as telepathy and second sight.

We were silent for quite some time.

"Is it now only among the Lapps that—"

"No! During the 1950s, I made a trip to a remote part of the Australian outback to visit a small tribe I'd heard about. I stayed several months. I made similar visits to very remote parts of the United States, Mexico, and South America—long enough to satisfy myself that this knowledge has survived among so-called primitive peoples."

"But what drove you to—"

"In Lapland, I should have died. Accidentally, I lived. It afforded me a unique opportunity to complete my task."

"What task?"

He gazed down at his feet, completely still, in deep concentration.

"If a man, by conscious effort or by accident, has acquired the conception of a soul, he must inevitably be born again and again into the same life. If he understands, however dimly, what he must do and does it, he can avoid his worst mistakes because he will begin to remember what happened last time."

"How can he begin to remember?"

"He has to have a very real hunger to discover a certain ancient knowledge that is deeply hidden. He has to pay a very high price in advance. Then, having found it, he has to make a lifelong effort, putting it first in his life. He can only do that if he has the strongest possible incentive."

"What would constitute as such an incentive?"

"All my life, especially during the War, I was conscious that, at any moment, I might die. I know of no greater incentive to make the effort required."

"And if you do not make this effort?"

"It takes many, many lives of continuous effort until the soul is perfected. Otherwise, it will suffer, and languish for eternity. Fortunately, there is an ancient knowledge, a teaching, which exists to help unfortunates in this position—unfortunates like you and me."

I found myself staring at him in astonishment.

"What do you mean like me?"

"You do not remember your other lives. But Aladdin's story made you weep like a child. Something deep inside you remembers and is calling to you, something you now have no direct access to."

He paused, and we both went into contemplative mode. Quietly, he lifted the long-handled ladle and poured water on the stones. With a choking sound, the steam arose, burning into our lungs.

"There's a story about a young man who came to Socrates and told him he wanted to acquire wisdom. 'Come with me,' said Socrates and took him to a river, where he shoved the surprised young man's head under the water until he fought his way back up, gasping for air. 'When you want wisdom as badly as you just now wanted air,' said Socrates, 'you will acquire it.'"

I looked at Sirel. I didn't see the point of the story, but he made no further comment.

"I accidentally discovered something many years ago—that we must learn to take in from the outside world and give out again one single impression. That way, we can begin to form something in ourselves that religions, from the beginning of time, have referred to as a 'soul.'"

"I just want to be a writer."

Sirel shook his head and smiled mysteriously.

"I recognize you. I was just like you. You have to begin to form something in you. Only then can life begin to have real meaning. That meaning can increase until the day you die. Otherwise, you pass your time on this earth, an animal dreaming, happy or unhappy. And you will die with about as much meaning as a dog in the street."

What Sirel had said, I found truly shocking.

"You said that to acquire the kind of knowledge you have access to that payment was necessary."

"I said that what comes first is a kind of hunger. You have that hunger."

"But how can I begin to pay—"

"Payment comes later. Remember Socrates? When you want to know what you need to know as badly as that young man, come and see me here in Finland."

Sirel was ready to get up and leave. I had many other questions, but I asked just one: "What about this old man in Paris?"

"Ivanovitch? He was my guide in everything—until his death in 1949."

⌒Ⓜ⌒

Epilogue

⟨※⟩

$\mathcal{B}$EGINNING IN JUNE 1991, I began paying regular visits to Sirel in Finland. Hilge got her money. She decided she wanted to spend her last years in Israel with Habermel. They now live in a beautiful villa near Haifa. I went to both St Petersburg and Moscow to view Schliemann's treasure. The artifacts certainly looked real to me, as did the funerary gold mask—now in Athens—known as Schliemann's Agamemnon.

About the Author

ᏬᎳᎳᎳ

J OHN GALWAY WAS born in Athlone on the river Shannon in 1944. After graduating from university, he worked in many European countries, returning to Ireland in 1980 with a young family. He began submitting articles, illustrated by his wife, to the *Irish Times*, Ireland's premier newspaper. Although these were very successful, the financial return was hardly enough to sustain a family, so he and his wife decided to convert the eighteenth-century Georgian house they had bought in County Galway into a residential centre for the teaching of English as a foreign language to business and professional people from Europe.

Of course, being in the heart of fox-hunting country, equestrian activities were part of every client's 'package,' as were trips along the river Shannon to the many places of historic interest, including Clonmacnoise, that great seat of learning in early Christian times.

These activities provided much of the material for the illustrated articles that he and his wife continued to produce.

This is his first novel. He was inspired to write it as a result of research he did for an Irish national radio (RTE) programme in 1984 with the putative leader of the Estonian Resistance during World War II.

Apart from the *Irish Times* articles, he has read his own short stories on RTE Radio 1. In addition, he has contributed to a variety of magazines over the years.